One
Friday
Afternoon

T.K. Chapin

One
FRIDAY
AFTERNOON

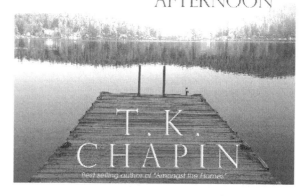

T.K.
CHAPIN

Best selling author of "Amongst the Flames"

ISBN-13:
978-1536908749

ISBN-10:
1536908746

DEDICATION

Dedicated to my loving wife.

For all the years she has put up with me

And many more to come.

CONTENTS

ACKNOWLEDGMENTS

First and foremost, I want to thank God. God's salvation through the death, burial and resurrection of Jesus Christ gives us all the ability to have a personal relationship with the creator of the Universe.

I also want to thank my wife. She's my muse and my inspiration. A wonderful wife, an amazing mother and the best person I have ever met. She's great and has always stood by me with every decision I have made along life's way.

I'd like to thank my editors and early readers for helping me along the way. I also want to thank all of my friends and extended family for the support. It's a true blessing to have every person I know in my life.

.

AUTHOR'S NOTE

Thank you for choosing to read **One Friday Afternoon**. I wrote this book to help inspire both men and women who are married or looking to marry to understand how much they need God in a relationship. A marriage is a three part relationship. You, the spouse and God. With divorce rates being so high even within the Christian community, I wanted to write a book that tackles real life head on. Real people with real problems that are happening in today's world. My hope is this story will bless you.

And we know that in all things God works for the good of those who love him, who have been called according to his purpose.
Romans 8:28

PROLOGUE

Decisions. They shape us into who we are and impact our lives in ways we often never realize. When I married Nathan, I was marrying my best friend and it was perfect. Our wedding was large and extravagant with all the trappings I had dreamed of as a little girl. Both friends and family came to usher us into the new chapter of our lives. Not long after the wedding, we decided to start a family.

Everything was falling into place, just like I had always dreamed that it would. Sure, we had disagreements and arguments, but they never lasted for long, and we always found ourselves apologizing by the end of them.

We were madly in love.

Three children later and almost twenty years of marriage, another decision came.

This time, it wasn't good.

My mistake came in a time of great weakness on my part. I had been struggling with losing my mother to cancer, and Nathan had been traveling on business for several weeks. One day at the local bookstore where I worked, one of my co-workers found me crying in the stockroom. I confided in him. From there, the emotional affair bloomed.

There's no excuse for what I did, and I know it was

my fault. For a long time, though, I didn't think that way. I didn't let myself take responsibility for what I had done.

Our selfishness in the flesh has a way of masking our eyes from the truth and blinding us of God's plan for our lives. I had myself convinced I committed my sin due to a lack of need in my marriage to Nathan. That wasn't true though. The real thing lacking in my marriage was God.

We, as humans, are capable of making horrible decisions and affecting not only our own lives, but the lives of others. Often, it happens without our knowing it until it's too late and the damage has already been done. If I could tell you one little Bible passage that flipped a switch in my soul and made everything better in my life, I would, but I can't. It was multiple verses and ultimately, my relinquishing control to God.

I'll tell you a story of how God took my broken marriage and made it beautiful. I'll show you how a single decision can change one's life forever.

CHAPTER 1

Speeding down the freeway, I could barely breathe between pauses in the argument from the passenger seat. It was infuriating that Nathan, my husband of eighteen years, *still* to this day could somehow forget to turn a coffee pot off. Though if I were being honest with myself, I didn't care about the coffee pot. No, it was how he made me feel—like he didn't care about me. If he couldn't turn off a coffee pot after I asked him this morning, how was this special getaway going to fix anything in our marriage?

"I already told you I'm sorry, Elizabeth! I don't know what more I can do here," Nathan said as he slammed the steering wheel with an open palm. Our special getaway was quickly derailing and becoming a full-on disaster in the making. My attempts to get through that thick skull were falling short. *He always does this. He ruins everything.* My negative thoughts crowded their way to the forefront of my mind and took the steering wheel. *How could any man care so little for everything in his life?* I wondered. It was incomprehensible and drove my hopelessness to new depths.

"Just think about something other than yourself," I said. "*Literally,* just have a thought outside of *you!* How about that?"

"It's a coffeemaker! C'mon!" he snapped, slamming the steering wheel again. "Why do you have to always freak out about nothing?"

"Fine." The conversation between us stopped, but it continued in my own thoughts. My dislike of Nathan was growing more each day, and hope was dwindling.

Turning my attention out the window, I saw pine trees blurred along the side of the road as I felt my chest tighten under the pressure of my heart breaking. *This trip is such a waste of time.* We were already one foot into the deep end of misery, and our two teenagers were stuck at my in-laws' over two hours away. *All the trouble of driving Jenny and Dakota to Moses Lake so we can spend our time away fighting in a fancy place?* The thought of being stuck in a room with that man for a week pained me.

Silence mingled with the tension between us the rest of the way to the bed and breakfast. As we pulled into the driveway of the inn, a woman opened the front doors and walked outside. She beamed with a smile that did nothing but annoy me. Instantly feeling bad by my annoyance, I pushed it aside and told myself, *have a good time. Just try. We don't know that Nathan will be a jerk the whole time, and we don't know what that doctor will end up saying.* A woman waved as Nathan slowed to a stop.

"Must be Serenah," Nathan said as he put the car into park.

I nodded. Without Nathan's knowledge, I made myself a promise that if this getaway didn't produce something of a change in our marriage, I'd be filing divorce papers once we got back to Spokane. It was a tall order to put on a simple stay at a bed and breakfast, but I needed something—anything—to change. I would not put up with him anymore.

"You must be the Collinses," she said as we got out of the car.

"That's us," I replied, extending a hand as we met her in the driveway. She beamed with that same smile. *What are you on, lady?* I wondered as I returned a forced, lesser smile. Noticing the gorgeous Diamond Lake behind her and the bed and breakfast, I suddenly cared a little less about everything. The beauty of the lake captured my attention.

Serenah turned around and peered out to the lake as she said, "It's stunning, isn't it?"

"Yeah," I said, my tone light and my mind a little less cluttered.

"Let me show you inside and give you a tour."

Serenah led us down the driveway and toward the house.

"I'll grab the bags. Go ahead, and I'll catch up."

Nathan went back to the car as we continued.

Following behind Serenah, we passed through the foyer. A see-through fireplace connected into the living room from the foyer caught my eye as I saw charred blackness on the fake wooden logs in the fireplace. Passing from the fireplace, my eyes saw in through the living room and the French doors that led out to a balcony that overlooked the lake. I couldn't help but keep looking at the lake as we turned out of the foyer and began up the stairs.

"How was the drive in?" she asked, pulling my attention away from the lake view.

"It was fine," I replied.

To that, she replied, "Good."

At the top of the stairs, there was a bedroom, then a walkway over to another room. Glancing over the railing, I could see down into the living room and through the large windows that hung above the French doors in the living room. "What a perfect view," I said. Serenah stood beside me at the railing and looked across the living room and toward the lake.

"It's amazing here. Every room has a view of the lake. I've been here over a year now and still can't get over it." Turning, she said, "It gets better. I've upgraded you guys to the best room in the house since nobody else had it booked during the time you're here. No extra charge."

"Thank you. Nathan will be thrilled."

She led me farther down the walkway and to the French doors at the end. When she opened them, I was overwhelmed to the point I had even forgotten about the fact that Nathan and I had fought the whole way here. A king size bed sat on one side of the room and a Jacuzzi on the other. Smells of cinnamon and vanilla tickled my nose as I walked farther into the room. My eyes found a set of French doors on the wall facing the lake. Taking a glance out the window, I saw a private balcony overlooking the lake. It reminded me of the night that Nathan and I had stayed in San Francisco on our honeymoon. We had a private balcony. We enjoyed our cups of coffee overlooking the city and talked about how all the people down below looked like ants.

"We provide breakfast and lots of coffee, but no other meals," Serenah said, pulling me out of the memory. I continued through the room as she spoke. "Newport isn't very far, and they'll deliver pizza and that kind of thing if you don't want to drive. A full list of places to eat and things to do can be found in the nightstand." Serenah flipped on the bathroom lights as she walked in behind me. High ceilings made the bathroom feel spacious, and a walk-in shower set the tone of luxury.

"This place is amazing," I said softly.

"*Elizabeth*," Nathan's voice echoed through the house and into the bathroom.

My face went red with embarrassment as Nathan hollered again through the house. "Sorry," I said to Serenah and hurried out of the bathroom and room, hurrying my steps out to the railing. I looked down at him and scolded him. "This isn't our house! You can't just yell."

He scoffed and shook his head as he looked up at

me. "Always picking apart what I do, aren't you?"

"I'm just saying that it's not our house and you can't

be yelling!" I tried to say in a loud whisper down to

him.

He stood there, shaking his head in disgust.

"Get on with it, Nathan. What did you want?" I

asked, placing my hands on the railing.

"Where's my razor? I didn't see it in the bathroom

bag. These whiskers coming in on my neck are

driving me nuts," he replied, scratching at his neck.

A sense of fear edged into my mind as I realized I

didn't pack it. "I must have forgotten it this morning

during all the chaos of last-minute packing. You

don't *need* to shave right now." Glancing at his

already scruffy facial hair, I knew he would be upset.

"Yes, I do need to shave, and what chaos? I loaded

the bags and got gas. All you did was pack a

bathroom bag and get in the car."

Before I could reply, Serenah stepped out of the bedroom and said, "No talk about the world out there. Just let yourselves relax. We have a convenience store up the road in Newport, and I'm sure they'll have a razor for you."

He smiled politely and nodded. "Thank you, Serenah."

He bent over and picked up the bags. "Where's the room?"

"I was just showing Elizabeth your room. I upgraded you to the best room in the house since we didn't have any other reservations. No extra charge."

Nathan's face lit up. "That's awesome!" he said, smiling at Serenah as he walked up the stairs with the bags in hand.

"Go ahead and get settled into the room," Serenah

offered. "I'll be downstairs, just past the foyer, in the kitchen. Oh, one other thing to note—there is Netflix on every TV in the house, but it's a shared account by all guests. I'm a devout born-again Biblical Christian and don't watch the majority of what you might see on the *Previously Watched* list. Lots of different people stay here."

"Okay," I replied. "We'll get settled and catch up with you in a bit. Thanks for everything." Her comment about her faith was a bit of a surprise, but comforting at the same time to me. Nathan and I hadn't been to church in almost four years, but we still held the values and beliefs of the Bible. "We're believers too," I added.

"That's awesome, and you're welcome," she said as she turned and headed downstairs.

Closing the door to our room as we got inside, I

turned around to Nathan. He tossed our bags onto the bed and fixed his eyes on the Jacuzzi. "This place is awesome. I'm so glad you decided to have us come here." He looked over at the TV on the dresser. "I can totally watch the NBA finals tonight from the Jacuzzi."

"Yay . . . I'm so excited," I said dryly.

He turned around and crinkled up a corner of his face. "It's do or die tonight. I have to watch it. You understand that."

Sighing, I shrugged. "Whatever." The truth was that it hurt. It hurt that instead of spending the first night with me and doing something fun in the little town of Newport or going down to the lake, he wanted to sit in the room and watch a basketball game. Going over to the mirror, I looked up at the ceiling and shook my head as I felt tears welling in my eyes. This place was amazing, and I feared the worst—nothing outside of a few arguments and a bunch of TV watching would be accomplished by the end of our trip. If the first few minutes at the inn were a precursor to how the trip would go, I might as well not even unpack my bag.

CHAPTER 2

Later that evening, after Nathan soaked in the

Jacuzzi for an hour, we were lying on the bed. My

hand was draped over his bare chest while we

watched the NBA finals game. One team had pulled

ahead so far in the lead by the third quarter that

there was little chance of the other team catching

up. Sliding my hand off his chest, I pressed my palm

against the bed and raised my body up to look Nathan in the eyes. "I'm getting hungry. Can we go into Newport and eat?"

Hesitating for a moment, he said, "You know I would, but I'm kind of watching this game, babe."

Furrowing an eyebrow, I glanced over at the television and let out a light laugh. "*Why?* Golden State is so far in the lead that there's no chance of anything changing."

He shrugged a shoulder and didn't so much as look over at me. "You never know what can happen. Just bring me something back. Cool?"

My heart felt like it was on a cliff and he just kicked it over the ledge. I felt so unloved, so unseen. *A silly basketball game is more important than spending time with me?* My natural reaction wasn't to show my hurt side and true side. It was, instead, an attempt to cripple him by belittling him, one insult at a time, in the hopes it'd get through to him.

"You're such a jerk!"

He shot a look over at me and lifted his hands out. Glancing around the room, he laughed. "This *jerk* got you a nice getaway, and you can't even let him watch a single basketball game for a few hours? Seriously, Elizabeth."

Tears began to well up in my eyes. Sliding off the bed, I hurried across the room and slipped on my flip-flops in a fury. Grabbing my purse off the dresser, I said, "*Fine*. I'll go by myself, as usual."

He jumped up from the bed and hurried across the floor. Stopping me with both hands on my arms, he looked me in the eyes. "Honey . . . don't let the emotions overtake you. I love you, and we'll do stuff. This game just means a lot to me."

I glared at him as I met his eyes.

He leaned forward and kissed my forehead.

"What do you want to eat?" I asked.

"Surprise me."

A stinging pain scraped across my heart as I left the room. He was selfish enough to stay and watch the game, but not so selfish that he couldn't address my anger in the moment. Finding myself in a quiet hallway on the other side of the door, I let my tense shoulders relax. I adjusted the shoulder strap of my purse and walked over to the stairs and headed down. As I came to the front door, I heard footsteps coming from the direction of the kitchen. I turned and looked to see who it was.

Serenah walked into the foyer with a load of folded laundry on her hip, but she turned the corner and headed downstairs.

"Hey," I called out.

"Yeah?" Serenah replied, pausing at the first step on the stairs leading down to the lower level.

"Would you . . . pray with me? You said you were a Christian earlier."

"Of course I'll pray with you," Serenah replied, setting the laundry basket down on the foyer floor. Walking over, she bowed her head and put her hand on my shoulder. Looking up at me, she said, "Anything in particular?"

Letting out a sarcastic laugh, I said, "My life. Sorry if that's a little forward of me."

"It's okay," she replied. Lowering her head, she prayed. "Dear God. I want to pray for Elizabeth right now. May your hand be upon her life and be with her situation at this moment. May you give her Your comfort that only You can provide. We also want to ask prayer that her time here at the inn is one of discovery and whatever else you want it to be. We love you, Jesus. Amen."

"Thanks," I said, raising my eyes as I wiped them. She did not understand what plagued my mind and heart, but her words rang true. Looking at her, I said, "I'm going to Newport. Did you need anything? Milk or something?"

Serenah shook her head and smiled. "No, but thank you for asking." Without any questions and with no judgment, Serenah returned to her basket of laundry and continued downstairs. Part of me wanted to confide in her about my marriage problems. Between that and the phone call I was waiting for from the doctor, I felt like I had the world on my shoulders. Going back over to the door, I opened it and left.

After grabbing a bite to eat, I decided to walk around downtown Newport. With the weather being so nice and my husband being preoccupied, I thought it was best to make use of the beautiful June evening. Peering into windows lining the sidewalk stores, I saw a random assortment. Dresses, shirts, toys, music instruments, and even some antiques sat in one window. A pet store was on the corner of Main Street. Stopping at the window, I saw a dozen or so puppies jumping around. A few were crawling over one another. The little furballs brought a smile to my face.

One of the puppies in the window stood out from the rest. Leaning in to get a closer look, I realized the pup reminded me of our old dog, Bandit. Nathan had picked him up shortly after our wedding and brought him home. He reasoned that we needed to try out raising a dog before we would try raising a child. Everyone knew I couldn't even keep a plant alive, and I was confident that Nathan was testing the waters by getting the dog. It was sweet of Nathan to protect my feelings that way. *What I wouldn't give to have that back.*

"Ma'am?" A little boy asked from beside me at the pet shop's window.

"Yes?"

"Could I interest you in a pastry? We have berry, orange, strawberry . . ."

Peering over the top of the little boy's box, I saw a wide-ranging variety, but the problem was that I wasn't hungry anymore. Glancing at his mother as she stood nearby, our eyes connected and she smiled at me with a familiar exhausted look in her eyes. *Poor gal,* I thought to myself. "I'd love a berry one. How much are they?"

"Two dollars, ma'am." The boy adjusted his footing and smiled back at his mom.

Fishing a couple of dollars from my purse, I handed it over to him and took my pastry. "Thank you."

"Thank you!" he replied and continued on down the sidewalk.

Taking my dessert with me, I went over to a patch of grass that held a little bench not far from the pet store. As I sat down on the bench, I set my purse down and crossed a leg. Peering across the street at a park where a mother was pushing her child on a swing set, I smiled thinking about how unique this little town truly was. Newport wasn't just a town near Diamond Lake. It was a secluded and peaceful community that was far enough away from a major city like Spokane to keep itself undisturbed by the realities of the world. It wasn't like Spokane, where you had to make sure there wasn't a group of homeless people camping out near the swing sets before you took your kids there. No, Newport was special. I could sense it in the air.

Arriving back at the inn that evening, I found Nathan dozing. He might have driven me nuts at times, but I still loved him. Setting my purse down on the dresser, I smiled. I thought about how peaceful and sweet he still looked after eighteen years of marriage. His lips did this thing where a bit of air would come out every time he would exhale.

Going over to the bed, I set his bag of food down on the night stand and climbed over to his chest. I let my head rest on his shoulder gently, knowing it would wake him.

"Hey . . ." he sleepily said a moment later. He adjusted and sat up in the bed. Rubbing his face over with his hand, he squinted at me.

"Here you go," I replied, turning and grabbing the bag off the nightstand.

He opened it up and pulled out a burger and fries.

"Where'd you get it from?"

"Dixie's Diner. I ate there earlier and it was good, so I stopped there on the way out of Newport."

He nodded and said, "Thanks."

He prepared to eat, and I got up off the bed and went over to the balcony doors. I was about to open the doors and go out when Nathan called out to me.

"Hey. I'm sorry about earlier." His empty apology did little to soothe my aching heart. Ever since my mistake, he had been a different person.

"If you were sorry, you wouldn't have done it, Nathaniel." Opening the doors, I went out onto the balcony for a breath of air. Looking up across the early evening sky, I tried to let the stillness come over me. A dark red danced alongside purples and pinks as the sun made its exit on the day in the distance.

Nathan opened the door and came out.

"I'll make it up to you tomorrow. We can go do something fun. I promise, Elizabeth. I'm really sorry for how I made you feel."

My eyes dropped from the sky as I went over to the railing, and they fell on Serenah below. I saw her walking with a man in the grass, down by the water.

Next to them, not more than a few paces, was a

paddle boat. "Let's go paddle boating."

"Okay," Nathan said confidently.

"*In the morning*," I said, turning around with a raised

brow. I knew he loved sleeping in on his days off,

and I didn't want to spend four hours waiting for

him to wake up. He cringed, but I stepped closer

and framed his jaw with my hand. "Please?" I asked.

Touching was one way I knew I could help motivate

my husband to come over to my side. It didn't work

for everything, but it did the trick most of the time.

He grinned. "Tomorrow. Early. We'll do it."

I returned his smile. "Thank you."

He returned inside, and I turned back to the lake.

My sights returned to Serenah and the mystery man.

They had made their way down the dock on the

property and were now sitting side-by-side. *Who is that?* I wondered. Seeing the man stand up, I leaned a little more on the railing and watched intently. He moved over and positioned himself behind her. I felt awkward watching. Then he wrapped his legs around the sides of her and scooted in close. His chest pressed against her back as he held her close. *Young love . . .* I thought wishfully. I thought about how Nathan used to do that when we were dating years ago. If Nathan could just be that way again . . . things could be so different.

CHAPTER 3

Waking to the smell of eggs and bacon lingering in the air the next day, I let out a yawn and stretched my arms. Refreshed didn't describe the way I felt that first morning waking up at *The Inn at the Lake*. Not waking once in the night, I had slept for what felt like a decade. Turning over in the bed, I looked at Nathan. His mouth was gaping open and a line of drool dripped onto his pillow. In my attempt to make the new day delightful, I took my hand and ran my fingers through his hair to wake him.

A grunt came from his lips as he shifted and turned his head away from me. "One more hour," he said before promptly digging his head under the covers.

Pushing his shoulder, I said, "Can't you smell those eggs and bacon coming from downstairs? Let's go eat."

Silence.

Climbing over his shoulder, I pulled the covers down from his face and reminded him of his words. "You promised."

Forcing an eye open, he turned and looked up at me. "Okay."

Jumping up from the bed, I ran into the bathroom. Running a quick brush through my hair to get the mess somewhat under control, I caught my reflection in the mirror. I was smiling. Pausing, I told myself, *today's going to be a good day. I know it.*

Coming back into the bedroom, my hopes were quickly squashed as Nathan had fallen back asleep.

"Get up, Nathan!" I demanded as I walked to the end of the bed. Pulling up the covers, I tickled one of his feet to get him moving. A reflex knee-jerk caused his leg to flail, and his foot caught my bottom lip, causing me to fall backward. He immediately jumped up and climbed to the edge of the bed to look at me.

"Ouch," I said as my eyes welled with tears and I brought my fingers to my lip.

Pulling my hand back, I saw there was a little blood. Furrowing my eyebrows, I stood up and headed into the bathroom.

"I'm sorry. It was a reflex," he said, climbing off the bed and following me into the bathroom. Taking a tissue from the counter, I dabbed my lip.

"It's fine. Let's go eat."

After breakfast, we packed a backpack with snacks and water bottles for the trip on the water in the paddle boat. As we were heading down to the shore, we spotted the same guy I saw Serenah with last night coming from the shed down by the lake.

"You a friend of Serenah's?" I asked as we came down into the yard and met him in the grass.

He smiled and extended a hand. "Something like that. We're engaged. Name's Charlie."

I shook his hand. "I'm Elizabeth, and this is my

husband, Nathan."

He nodded and shook Nathan's hand. "Serenah said she had a couple check in last night. You two enjoying your time here?"

"Had a delicious breakfast, an amazing night's sleep, and no children. So yeah, I'd say it's going pretty well," Nathan replied with a grin.

"Good."

Glancing at the sky, Nathan said, "Those clouds aren't looking too promising, babe."

My eyes saw the lingering gray clouds above that held traces of darkness in them. "We'll be okay."

Charlie said, "Were you thinking the paddle boat or canoe? Because this paddle boat has a hole and won't be ready for the water until tomorrow."

"The canoe will be fine," Nathan said.

"We don't know how to canoe though," I said.

"It can't be hard. We'll figure it out."

"All right," I replied with skepticism in my voice.

Tipping over wasn't appealing, but I wasn't going to argue with him over it.

"I'd better get to fixing this," Charlie said.

"Sounds good, Charlie," Nathan replied. "It was nice meeting you." Nathan and I walked down the shoreline to the canoe. Nathan went over and started to drag the canoe while I gazed across the lake to the tall standing tree line that separated the bed and breakfast from the property next door. Peering through the trees, I could see a smaller tree standing alone in an opening in the woods. *What is that?* I wondered as I stepped toward the property line.

"Give me a hand with this," Nathan said, breaking my concentration.

Going over to the canoe, I helped push it off the yard and into the water. As my feet touched the water, chills ran up my spine and sent a shiver through my body. "Brr," I said as we both glided the canoe farther into the water.

Nathan took another look at the clouds, but quickly looked back at me. "Little chilly. Sure hope it's fine."

"It will be," I said confidently, but secretly, I was worried about it. Grabbing on the edge of the canoe, I hoisted myself up and in.

"Head to the other end. That's the front. Try to keep low so it doesn't tip."

Nodding, I kept low and moved to the front. *Maybe he has been canoeing before? Sounds like he knows what he's talking about.* At the front of the canoe, I set the bag down and sat. Picking up a paddle, I turned and watched Nathan get in. His skeptic eyes glanced up again at the clouds.

"Stop looking at the clouds, Nathan. It'll be fine."

"Just don't want to get stuck out in the middle of the lake in a downpour."

We paddled out into the lake and made our way farther away from *The Inn at the Lake*. As we went farther around the lake, we saw a massive house with two docks, jet skis, a boat and an in-ground swimming pool with a slide that wrapped around a deck from the house. "Now that's a house," Nathan said from the back of the canoe.

"A bit overkill," I said over my shoulder to him.

"Unless you have lots of friends." Almost kicking myself for the rude comment, I quickly apologized.

"Sorry." Nathan wasn't one to have many friends, and he often made it a point to avoid social gatherings of any kind. He found forms of friendship in reading and working on his stamp collection alone in his study at home. His work as an advertising consultant at BBSI often kept him late at the office, which also left little room for friends.

"It's okay," he replied. We paddled for another fifteen minutes on the lake and then suddenly, a sprinkle of rain began to fall.

Nathan said, "See."

Holding out my palm, I said, "It's barely a sprinkle." As the words fell from my lips, the clouds opened up and a downpour started. My jaw clenched. Nathan didn't have to say anything, but that didn't stop him.

"This is so stupid, Elizabeth. You know, if we just did what I wanted to do, we wouldn't have issues like this. I'm so sick of doing whatever you want to do."

Jerking my head around, I stood up in the pouring rain and said, "What I want to do? When we went on a family vacation last year, where did we go?

That's right. We went to Moses Lake to see *your*

parents. Not to Florida to see mine, and not to

Yellowstone to just have fun."

"Sit down, please," Nathan said, putting his hand

out.

"No!" I shouted. Stepping closer, I stuck out a finger

and said, "When the Librams wanted us to join them

on the road trip to Utah to Moab for the weekend to

go four-wheeling, did we go? No! We didn't go

because you didn't want to be around them. You

don't ever want to be around anyone." I shook my

finger as I took another step toward him.

The canoe rocked and toppled over.

Water rushed around me and I swam to the surface.

Frantically looking around in the water, I shouted,

"Nathan!" The rain was pouring so hard that it was

difficult to see. Pushing my hair out of my face, I jerked my head left and then right. *Where is he?* My heart pounded.

"Elizabeth!" he shouted as he came around the canoe. "Grab the canoe and shove it over," he said firmly as he gripped the edge.

I grabbed on. Pushing it over in unison, we were able to flip it right-side up. Swimming over to me, he went under the water and helped me up into the canoe. Turning around, I grabbed his arm and helped him in. He looked me over intently as his hands held my face. His eyes were full of worry as the rain continued to pour. "Are you okay?" he asked.

"Yeah," I replied. My heartbeat started to calm, and all I could see was the rain pouring off his face and his hair. "I love you."

45

He smiled and sat back in the canoe, letting his body relax against the inner wall as we waited for the rain to settle. "I love you too," he said gently. Not more than a few minutes more, the rain let up.

As we climbed back to our seats, he said, "You know, Elizabeth. I don't know why I'm the way I sometimes am with you."

Nathan talking? What is this? I wondered. It wasn't a usual side for him to show. "What do you mean?"

He shrugged. "I just don't trust you, and oftentimes, I don't really like you. Really . . . I don't know what's wrong with me."

A dagger to the heart. I dipped my chin and stayed quiet.

Nathan shook his head and sighed heavily, looking back over at me. "I want things back the way they were a long time ago. Before all that. You know . . .

when I thought you were perfect."

I remained silent, but my tears screamed. I always wanted him to talk about it, get it all out, but now, I regretted that. Maybe I truly didn't want to know how he felt. It hurt too much. He worked his way over to me in the canoe. Pulling my chin up with a finger, he looked into my eyes. "I'm still here."

"But are you really?" I asked gently, my eyes bouncing between both of his.

"What?" he asked, almost surprised. Turning his head toward the way back to the inn, he said, "We should get back to the inn and get into some dry clothes."

He returned to his seat, and we paddled the rest of the way back to the inn without words between us. Though we had talked, I felt worse than I did before.

CHAPTER 4

Returning to the inn and getting into dry clothing,

Nathan took off to buy a new razor in town and

something for lunch for both of us. I had a headache

and didn't want to go anywhere at the moment. Five

minutes after he left, the headache coincidentally

vanished.

Leaving our room, I headed downstairs and out to

the balcony on the main level. The clouds had cleared and the sun was out. I wanted to soak up some rays and relax. Nathan voicing his concern for my not being perfect drew me into a depressing reality—we didn't stand a chance if he wanted perfection.

"Enjoying that sunshine?" Serenah asked, coming out through the open French doors off the dining area.

Glancing over my shoulder at her from the lounge chair I was in, I replied, "Yeah. It seems to have cleared up beautifully."

"That rain earlier was pretty intense. I'm glad you two made it back safely." She walked over to a nearby chair and sat down. Peering out across the water, she asked, "Was it fun?"

Laughing with a sarcastic breath of air, I replied,

49

"Yeah. Something like that. Hey, that reminds me. We met your man down by the water."

"Oh, did you meet Charlie?" Serenah's face lit up. "He's my sweetheart. Must have been here fixing that paddle boat again."

"Yeah, he was. Seems like a really nice guy. How'd you two meet?"

"We met at Dixie's Diner unofficially when I was working there, but we met here at the inn officially. I was working a part-time job for the owner last summer. We've been dating over a year now."

"Love at first sight?" I asked, smiling.

"Maybe lust, but not love. Enough about me. Where'd your beloved go?"

Relaxing my head back against the lounge chair's head rest, I said, "Off to get a razor and some lunch."

"Sorry. I didn't mean to pry."

"No. It's fine. You're not prying."

"I saw your cut lip at breakfast. You okay?"

I laughed. "That was just an accident. I'm more upset that life just isn't going the way I dreamed it would go. Oops. Did I just say that?" I asked, lifting my head to look at her. "I didn't mean to—"

"You're fine. I love girl talk. Life doesn't usually go the way we think it should go. Or at least, it doesn't a lot of the time. I think God does work it all for good in the end though." Serenah hesitated to continue, but then she did anyway. "I don't usually tell people this, but my ex-husband abused me. I was devastated. It took a long time for me to leave him, but I did. A year later, I met Charlie and was asked to run this inn. Though I've been in counseling for a couple of years now as a result of John, I can see where God's hand was over my life.

51

God's always working and shaping our lives in ways
we don't fully understand."

"Wow. That's neat that it all worked out for you."
With her revealing an intimate part of her life, I felt
comfortable opening up. "Nathan and I have been
struggling for three years now."

"I sensed something there."

"Yeah. I made a mistake three years ago and had an
emotional fling with a guy, and Nathan never got
over it. He still doesn't trust me to this day."
Pressing my hand against my forehead, I said, "I
don't know why I'm telling you this."

"Can we pray?" Serenah asked.

"Yeah. I'd like that."

She placed her hand on mine and prayed out loud.
"Dear God. We come to Your throne room this
beautiful day and lift up to You Elizabeth and

Nathan and their marriage. We know You are working continuously for us, and we call upon the promise of Your Word that tells us all things work together for good for those who love you and are called according to Your purpose. Please let Your Will be done in this marriage and in their lives. In Your heavenly name, we pray, Amen."

Lifting my eyes, I looked to Serenah and said, "Thank you. We used to go to church so much more when the kids were younger, but it just . . . slowed down. You know?"

"It's often a slow fade," Serenah replied. "Church is good and can be beautiful, but it's only an addition to the relationship we already have in Christ. We don't go to church to get Jesus, but instead go in obedience of His Word that plainly states not to forsake the assembly." Hearing someone open the front door, Serenah excused herself and went inside.

Her words lingered behind with me as I thought

back to the times Nathan and I had been attending

church regularly. I longed for the fellowship of other

believers who were like-minded, and a deep

yearning set into my soul. I was thirsty on a spiritual

level without knowing it. *I miss God,* I thought to

myself.

Serenah came back and sat down in her seat. "Just

the FedEx guy."

"How do I get Nathan to go back to church with me?

Any ideas?" I asked, hoping she'd be able to provide

insight into the matter.

Shaking her head, she said, "Don't worry about

Nathan. Focus on you, Elizabeth. Let God lead *you*."

Later that evening, Nathan and I headed into town
to eat at Dixie's Diner. As we took our seats in a
booth, a server came over. "Good evening. I'll be
your server tonight. My name's Miley. You two new
to town? Don't believe I've seen you in before."

"Yes," I replied. "We're staying out at *The Inn at the
Lake.*"

Miley's face lit up. "*The Inn at the Lake*? My friend,
Serenah, runs that place."

"She's a sweetheart. Really easy to talk to one-on-
one."

"Sounds like she's doing great. She really does have a
heart of gold," Miley replied. "What can I get you
two to drink?"

"I'll take a cola," Nathan said as his eyes stayed fixed
on the menu.

"Water, please," I said, making eye contact with her.

"Great. I'll be back in a few with those drinks and see if you're ready to order." Miley left the table.

Looking over the menu for a few moments, I stopped and lowered it to look at Nathan. My mind had been on God ever since my conversation with Serenah, and I wanted to test the waters out with where his heart was. "What do you think about going to church when we get back home?"

He peered up from his menu and raised an eyebrow. "You know the Thompsons still go there. After what they did to the Gillroys, I wouldn't feel—"

"Nathan," I interrupted. "Why does that matter? It happened four years ago."

He set the menu down on the table and brought his hands together. "*Well* . . . it mattered to *you* at one time. Wait, what's going on with you? Where did all this come from?"

Before I could speak, the server returned with our drinks and pressed about ordering.

"Give us about ten minutes," Nathan said curtly. He watched her walk away and then fixed his gaze on me. "Out with it, Elizabeth."

"I was just talking to Serenah earlier about us, and . . ."

"Excuse me? What does that mean? *Us?*"

"About how we've been having problems and—"

"No," he interrupted. Adjusting in his seat, he leaned across the table and said, "You told this stranger about what, exactly?"

"Just that we have been struggling. It's not a big deal." I shook my head, but my pulse raced as I could see Nathan come unglued.

He stood up and said, "I can't believe you." Pulling a

twenty out of his wallet, he dropped it on the table and headed for the exit. My eyes watered. On his way out of the restaurant, he almost ran into Miley, but he side-stepped her and went out the door in a rage.

"Just keep the money on the table," I said to Miley as she came over. Getting up from my seat, I wiped my eyes.

"You sure? You didn't have any—"

I walked past her in pursuit of Nathan. Once out on the sidewalk, I surveyed the road and spotted him across the street, walking with his head down and his hands in his pocket. Glancing both directions, I crossed over to the other side of the road. Catching up to him, I touched his shoulder to stop him.

"Can I not have a moment alone?" he snapped as he stopped and turned. "Just five minutes. Or is that too much to ask?"

I bit my lip as tears trickled down my cheeks. He turned and continued walking down the sidewalk and vanished around the corner. Finding a nearby bench, I took a seat and prayed. *What am I supposed to do, God?* Then a quiet thought pressed against my mind like an invasion on my consciousness.

Tell him about the biopsy.

My heart hardened. Telling him about the biopsy would only create fear, worry and stress he didn't need. There was no reason for it. It was just standard procedure. Nathan worrying about the remote possibility of cancer wasn't really needed. My plan was to tell him once the doctor called with those test results in the next day or two.

Tell him about the biopsy, the thought pressed again, this time louder.

Though I had done such a great job at keeping it off my mind, it made a vengeful and quick appearance to the forefront of my thoughts. I knew God didn't talk to people, but it sure felt like He brought that thought to the tip of my mind.

Nathan texted me a while later and said he'd take a cab back to the inn when he was done thinking. His behavior reminded me more of a child than a grown man these days. Once I made it back to the inn, I took a walk down to the shore to clear my head. The sun was beginning to set across the evening sky and painted a postcard-worthy view of yellows and oranges that were impossible not to be in awe of. The yellows and reds above reflected off the smooth surface of the lake and filled my being with a much-needed sense of tranquility. Though everything felt a bit chaotic at that moment in my life, I felt at peace. As I peered across the waters and took a seat at the end of the dock, I thanked God for the day. After my prayer of thanksgiving, I couldn't help but feel bad for all the days I had missed in the last four years since we left church. *What happened to me?* I wondered. Then Serenah's words echoed in my ears, 'it's a slow fade.' Breaking into my thoughts, I heard conversation stirring about somewhere behind me in the distance. I looked. Charlie and Serenah were out on the main level balcony, enjoying each other's company. When I laid eyes on them, I saw Charlie brushing a strand of hair behind her ear.

Turning my sight back to the lake, I thought about Nathan. I wondered where he was and what he was doing and thinking about. *Why'd he freak out about that?* I asked myself. Dipping my chin to my chest, I started in on another prayer. *I don't know what to do, Lord.* My eyes began to well with tears as I felt hopelessness edge its way into my heart, causing my chest to tighten.

"Hey," Serenah's voice caught me off guard from behind.

Turning my eyes back to her, I nodded. "Hey."

Sitting down on the end of the dock beside me, she pulled her knees up to her chest and placed a hand on my back. "You okay? I don't mean to bother you. I can leave."

I shrugged. "It's no bother." Wiping my eyes, I shook my head and said, "I'm *fine*. Nathan's just upset I told you about our struggles."

"Ahh . . . yes. The male ego. It's an amazing thing,"

she replied as she shook her head and looked to the sky.

"Do you think divorce could ever be the answer? I know you're younger than me, but I'm just kind of curious what you think." My eyes trained on Serenah as I waited for a response.

"God never designed divorce—only marriage. Though he allows it, that was only due to humanity's sin." She paused and looked at me. "The Bible tells us to focus on the good. Right? Whatever is pure, whatever is of good report. Think on these things. Forget divorce and think about restoration . . . if you can."

"Serenah. The water is boiling," Charlie called down from the balcony.

"Be right there," she replied over her shoulder as she made eye contact with him on the balcony. Pushing herself up by her palms, Serenah stood and said, "I'll keep you in my prayers, Elizabeth."

"Thank you," I replied.

As she walked down the dock to return to the inn, I thought about the word she used. Restoration. *Restore . . . restore what? The closeness we once had. The intimacy that is nothing but a distant memory.* Focusing my thoughts on the early part of our relationship, I let my mind linger there for a moment. Recalling the night that I knew I'd someday marry Nathan, I smiled.

I could almost smell the Mexican food in the air from that evening and feel my bare feet gliding across the smooth stone dance floor as he flung me about passionately under the multicolored lights overhead. It wasn't the salsa dancing, the food or even the compliments he showered me with that made me know I would marry him. It was the conversation at the table after the last dance. The table wasn't over three feet in diameter, and he placed a hand over the top of mine as he leaned in. Looking into my eyes underneath the reds, greens and yellows from the lights of the dance floor, he spoke love into my soul. He told me about how much family meant to him. He told me how he dreamed of having kids, a wife, a house and a dog name Spanky that gets out of the yard through a broken board in the fence. He wanted it all. His voice trembled that night as he spoke, but it didn't stop me from feeling moved by every word that came from his mouth. I found out years later that he was scared to reveal that part of himself. It was a hidden part of him he didn't share with other girls. Just me. Smiling as the memory came to a stop, I gazed across the lake. *That old Nathan could have really enjoyed this place.*

My mind allowed that same pressing thought from earlier to press against my consciousness again. *Tell him about the biopsy.*

My heart softened this time. My restoration, my marriage's salvation could only happen if I made myself vulnerable and told him about the biopsy. I was fearful. *What if he doesn't care?* My worried mind asked. *What if he just says I'm fine and overdramatic?* Dipping my chin back to my chest as I felt my chest tightening up, I prayed for God to help me.

CHAPTER 5

The next morning, I awoke to Nathan sitting on the

edge of the bed opposite me. Fully clothed in the

same thing he wore yesterday, he was hunched over,

wringing his hands as he looked out the open

French doors that led out to the balcony. There was

something definitely wrong with him.

"Nathan?" I asked, sitting up. Reaching my hand

over, I touched his shoulder.

He turned on the bed to face me. His eyes were red and swollen. Licking his bottom lip, he pulled it in and bit as he looked hesitant to speak. Nathan's eyes were weary, but they carried a sadness I hadn't seen before. It was deep. He took my hand and placed it in his palm, then brought his other hand over top.

"Elizabeth . . ." He took a deep breath in and exhaled. "I don't know how to say this."

Scooting across the comforter closer to him, I said, "You can tell me anything, Nathan."

"I spent the evening walking around Newport and did a lot of thinking. Thought about you, the kids and really *everything* in my life. I know things have been hard these last few years and we've really grown apart. To imagine our life to be perfect was pure foolishness on my part."

My heart warmed. Nathan realized that I couldn't be perfect. He had come back to proclaim his unyielding love for me and apologize for being so distant in our marriage.

Before I could say anything, he continued, "This marriage just feels hopeless and doomed."

My heart went from feeling like I was on top of a mountain to freefalling to the earth in a ball of fire. *Hopeless? Doomed?* My throat clenched shut and my eyes instantly watered. The room, including Nathan, turned into a blur behind the teardrops of reality.

"Please don't cry," he pleaded as he squeezed my hand. "Haven't you felt that way? Even once?"

Though I had felt that way for some time, it didn't lessen the pain of his mentioning it. I nodded as I wiped my eyes. Pushing out a few quick breaths, I was composed enough to speak. "To be honest with you, yes. I have. In fact, I only wanted to come here to see if we could fix our marriage. But I realized something yesterday."

He raised his eyebrows, encouraging me to continue.

"What about God, Nathan? What does *He* want for our marriage?"

Letting out a sigh, Nathan turned on the bed toward the doors out to the balcony. He was quiet for a moment. Then he said, "God wants us to be happy, Elizabeth."

"Happy?" I shook my head. "I don't recall that part of the Bible. Joy, yes, but not happy."

Turning to me, he shook his head. "Things have happened that I don't think *we* can ever get past."

His tone was sharp. Definitive.

"Okay. Then just do it. Leave. You've already wasted

three years of my life, the kids' lives, and your own. Just do it. Go file the papers and be done with me already!" My phone rang on the nightstand, breaking through our conversation. Leaning over to see the caller ID, I saw it was the doctor. My heart felt like it skipped a beat. Reaching over, I silenced it. *Please don't ask, please don't ask.*

"Who was it?" Nathan asked.

Shaking my head, I knew I couldn't tell him. Not right now. He'd use it against me somehow.

"Nobody."

Rising to his feet, he came around the end of the bed as I stood. "Elizabeth. Who was that on the phone?" he asked, pointing to the nightstand like I had forgotten the location of it. "Was it Derek?"

"Of course not, Nathan! It was just a doctor for Jenny."

"What's going on with Jenny?" he asked, stepping closer. He looked concerned about his daughter now. I was digging a hole quickly.

I was about to start in on the lie, but that same tortuous thought from yesterday invaded my thoughts yet again.

Tell him about the biopsy.

I looked at him with tears in my eyes, my heart pounding against my ribcage and a fear he'd crush me if I said a word. Lifting my hand to my forehead as my breath drew shallow, I shook my head.

"Nathan . . ." His name tumbled out of my mouth, trembling as it left my lips.

His eyes widened as he came closer. He sensed something was wrong by my action. Worry scattered across his face as he touched my hand with his.

"What's going on?"

My eyebrows went up, and I had to wrangle and force each word that followed. "I had a mammogram a few weeks back." I bit my lip as I struggled to continue. I could feel my throat clench, and everything inside me tried to stop me from speaking more, but I did. "They found a lump, Nathan."

As Nathan's face grimaced, I felt the sting of his pain course through me. He began to cry, sending my heartache for him further into my soul. Glancing at my chest for a second and then back into my eyes, he covered his mouth with his hand.

I continued, "They did a biopsy four days ago. I've been waiting on the test results—"

Tears poured from his eyes as he closed the remaining distance between us. I hadn't seen him cry more than once or twice in our lives together. Pulling me into his arms, he grabbed me in an embrace.

We cried together.

After a few moments passed, we wiped our eyes and it was if a different man stood in front of me. Nathan wasn't the same. He kept looking at me, like he hadn't seen me in a long time. Then he asked, "Why didn't you tell me?"

"I didn't want to worry you."

His jaw trembled as more tears started. Shaking his head, he said, "I'm so sorry I made you feel like that. I want you to be able to tell me anything."

"You're not mad?" I asked.

He shook his head as his hand framed my face. His eyes looked so worried, so concerned. A part of him was revealed that I thought was gone like the days of our youth. "No, honey. I'm not mad." His eyes turned to the nightstand. "So was that the doctor calling with the results?"

I nodded.

We went over, and I grabbed my phone to call them back. As the phone rang on speaker, Nathan kept looking into my eyes. His gentle touch against my arm made me feel safe. The newfound care I saw in him was bizarre and not at all what I had expected.

"Dr. Hammer's office, how can I help you?" the receptionist answered.

"Hi, this is Elizabeth Collins. I had a biopsy done on Thursday, and I think someone tried calling with the results."

"Just a moment while I place you on hold."

As the music came on the line, Nathan began crying again. Placing a hand on his shoulder, I said, "It's going to be okay, Nathan."

Though I was freaked out about it as much as he

was, I could keep myself composed. My initial reaction when they found the lump during the mammogram was a different story. I had lost all control of my emotions right there in the doctor's office and cried hysterically. A nurse even had to calm me down.

"Mrs. Collins?" the receptionist came back on the line saying.

"Yes."

"Let me transfer you back to the nurse."

The phone rang as my thoughts raced. *If it was okay, she would have just told me. This isn't good.* Nathan wrapped his arm around me and pulled me in tight as we waited for what felt like an eternity.

"This is Betty. This Elizabeth?"

"Yes," I replied curtly.

"The biopsy came back fine. We'll want to keep an

eye on it, but for now, you're okay." As she continued on about the need for regular self-examination and keeping annual appointments in the future, my mind went straight to the throne room of God. *Thank you, Lord. Thank you.* Nathan rubbed my shoulder and wept into it as we both breathed a heavy sigh of relief.

After getting off the phone, I turned to Nathan. Expecting to see a smile, I saw something else. He looked conflicted. "What's wrong?" I asked, touching his arm gently. "I thought this would be a time of celebration and happiness."

He pinched the bridge of his nose with his thumb and index finger as he looked down and continued to cry. "I'm so, so happy about the results . . ."

Furrowing my eyebrows, I shook my head. "Then what's the problem?"

He lifted his eyes to meet mine. "I . . . I didn't know how much I still loved you, Elizabeth. I did something bad. *Really* bad."

Worry soared through every inch of my body. "What did you do? Did you have a drink in Newport?"

He shook his head and turned. Walking out to the balcony, he rested his hands on the railing outside. He dipped his head between his arms as if the world rested on his shoulders. Following him outside, I placed my hand on his back. "Talk to me."

He lifted his eyes to look at me. Tears streamed down his cheeks as he held a look of fear behind his eyes. "I cheated on you."

"What?" My moment of joy quickly faded and shock took over me.

He shook his head, and more tears came down his cheeks as he wiped them away.

"When? With whom?" I demanded.

"I don't want to talk about it."

Anger and wrath consumed me. I shoved him, and he lost his footing. "I don't care if you don't want to talk about it, Nathan! You're going to talk about it right now. Tell me."

He raised his hands up and said, "It lasted only a month, a long time ago. After Derek. It's over now. We both have made mistakes here."

"You hid it from me all this time?" I asked. Pressing my hand against my forehead, my shock turned into a deep anger.

"I'm so sorry," he replied, bringing his hands up to touch my arms.

I stepped back. I asked, "Was it Stacy? From the Christmas party? The one I saw you talking to and she was laughing hysterically at your lame Santa joke?"

"No. It was a girl in accounting. Melissa. Look, it was a long time ago, and I don't want anything to do with her."

"What did you do with her? Was it physical or emotional?"

He dipped his head in shame.

"It's over." Turning, I left the balcony and went inside. Tears came as I crossed the floor to the bathroom. *How could he?* I slammed the bathroom door shut and locked it. Walking up to the mirror, I gazed at my swollen red eyes and the tears running down my face. *Is this what I deserve? I make one mistake, so he goes out and cheats on me?* My bottom lip trembled. *What now, God? What now?* Glancing over at Nathan's new razor, I picked it up and broke it in half. *Shave now, jerk!*

A knock came from the door.

"Go away, Nathan," I shouted over my shoulder.

"C'mon, Lizzy . . . let me in." The nickname strummed a chord in my heart that hadn't been touched in years. He hadn't called me that since we were courting, almost two decades ago. *How dare he use that name right now.*

Scoffing, I went over to the door and opened it.

"What, Nathaniel? What do you want? You want to justify to me how you only did what you did because of me?"

"No . . ." He stepped closer and touched both my arms, causing me to become nauseas as I thought of him with his floozy. Worming out of his touch, I took a step back.

"Don't touch me."

His eyes widencd and welled with tears.

"How could you touch me after all you have done with *her*? I don't want to see you. Please leave me alone and go do something."

He shook his head. "*Fine.* Don't forget what you said about what God wants here. Or maybe you only said that because it worked in your favor at the time?"

Frustrated at his accusations, I grabbed onto the edge of the door and swung it shut in his face. Collapsing on the bathroom floor, I folded into my palms and cried. As more tears poured down my cheeks, I felt my eyes become heavy as if I could sleep. Lying down against the cold tiles of the bathroom, I let the side of my face rest against the coolness. My sadness was too much to handle, and my eyes closed.

CHAPTER 6

A few hours passed and I awoke. As I stood up, I rubbed the back of my neck and peered over at the mirror. A part of me felt gone. What was left was a sad and empty woman who felt her world crumbling around her. Seeing my hair, I shook my head as my attention shifted to it. My hair was a mess. I walked over to the sink and splashed water on my face and ran a brush through my hair. Nathan's infidelity pelted against my mind with every passing minute. I gave my heart to that man, and he smashed it like a bug. Not only did he cheat, he carried it with him for years before telling me. *How many times did he meet with her? Did they go out together? Ugh.* My eyes couldn't help but water at the thoughts. It felt like I was in a nightmare with no way to wake up. We still had days left at the inn, but I wasn't going to wait to leave. Another night at this place with him would surely kill me. I needed to get back to Spokane and file for divorce as soon as I could.

Coming out of the bathroom, I saw all his clothing were gone and a note on the bed. Picking up the piece of paper, I read it.

Lizzy,

I know my words carry little weight right now, but I'm truly sorry. If you give me a chance, I'll make this right—God willing. Meet me at Dixie's Diner in Newport at four o'clock for dinner. I left because I figured you didn't want me here right now.

Love,

Nathan

"Really?" I asked, dropping the note back on the bed.

Grabbing the duffel bag from across the floor, I began to pack all my clothing. As I rounded up my final few miscellaneous items around the room, a knock came from the door.

Leaving the duffel bag on the bed, I went over and opened it.

It was Serenah.

"Do you need any towels?" she asked. I saw her eyes gravitate to my duffel bag on the bed.

"I'm going to check out early and go home."

Serenah nodded and said, "Is everything okay?"

My heart pounded, and tears instantly welled in my eyes. I shook my head.

She stepped into the room and set the towels on the end table. Putting an arm around me, she said, "It's okay."

"No it's not," I cried as I lay my head on the practical stranger's shoulder. "My marriage is over."

Shaking her head, Serenah looked at me. "Only if you allow it to be."

"No. It's too far gone, Serenah. You don't even know. He—"

She grabbed my hand and said, "I don't need to know the details of what's happened. I know the

Author of love and Inventor of marriage. I'm not trying to make you stay with a bad man, and I really feel odd saying all this because we don't really know each other, but it was pressed onto my heart to speak with you just now. That's why I brought the towels. At the very least, go to God before you make a decision."

"Don't feel weird about it. I know God uses people all the time." I let out a sigh and nodded. "I will pray about it, but I won't promise anything."

She smiled. "I don't expect you to promise me or anybody anything at all, Elizabeth. I'll be down in the kitchen. If you decide to leave, just stop by and let me know." As she walked out the door, I shut the door quietly behind her and then sat on the bed. Bringing my hands together, I prayed. I asked God for wisdom in the situation at hand. As I finished, I felt an overwhelming desire to open my Bible app on my phone and read Ruth—an old favorite book in the Bible that I hadn't read in quite some time. After finishing the book of Ruth, I turned the screen off and combed over the story in my mind. *How did Ruth have so much faith in such uncertain times?* Ruth's husband had died, and she technically had no obligation to stay with her mother-in-law, Naomi, but she did. Naomi even permitted her to leave, but Ruth never left. She stayed. Though Ruth wasn't in a marriage with Naomi, she put trust in God over the situation. In the end, it not only worked out for her, but she was blessed.

Quieting my mind, I closed my eyes and stretched out on the bed, letting my eyes focus on the ceiling as a small breeze blew through the open doors leading out to the balcony. In the distance, I could hear the faint sound of boats zipping by on the lake, but I remained focused on slowly quieting each part of my heart and mind.

Once cleared, I didn't let another thought in, and I focused on remaining as still as possible as I closed my eyes. Minutes passed by, and my mind decided on its own to jump from nothingness to Nathan. My heart felt a jolt of pain rip through. It hurt to think about him.

The pain was so intense I could barely stand it, but I let it come over me.

Sadness.

Fear.

Hurt.

Guilt.

Sitting up quickly on the bed, I turned and looked out the open doors. All the intensity of emotions faded into the back of my mind.

Getting up, I walked out onto the balcony for a breath of clean summer air. Surveying the lake, my eyes eventually fell to the shoreline of the inn. I saw the canoe and thought about our trip on the water the other day. The yelling, the tipping over. Most of it was my own fault. *How much am I responsible for his stepping out on me in our marriage?* I wondered. *Would he have done it if I'd never had that emotional fling with Derek?* I pondered. Turning back to the room, I saw the letter on the bed. The idea of seeing that man again stung in the recesses of my soul, but he was still my husband and I needed to hear what he had to say.

The rest of the day leading up to my meeting with Nathan was spent praying, reading my Bible app, and watching as patrons of the lake sped across the water. While everyone seemed to be out partaking in the summertime activities, I was seeking God. The same God that had gotten me through the better part of my life and into my marriage. Though it wasn't my fault that Nathan did what he did, I couldn't help but feel a sense of guilt over the lack of relationship I had with God. And though Nathan and I left the church because of drama, I realized it was much more than that. After Nathan began making more money in life, my prayers slowed and my reliance on God dwindled too. Though my day brought a lot of confusion, what I did know by the time my cab arrived to pick me up for dinner was that I needed God more than ever. Whether I stayed

with Nathan or we ended up separating, I needed
God back in my life, and this time, forever.

"Dixie's Diner in Newport, right?" the cab driver
asked as I climbed into the back.

"Yes, please." Looking out the window, I saw a bird
flying from a tree branch out in the yard of the inn.
The verse from Matthew 6:26 I read earlier pressed
against my mind. *They do not sow or reap or store
away in barns, and yet your Heavenly Father feeds
them. Are you not much more valuable than they?*
Knowing God was with me regardless of what I do or
say or the way I act brought a comfort to me that
was not of this world. My own sin-riddled mind was
attacking me almost simultaneously as the Lord was
helping me, but the fiery darts of the enemy would
not stand a chance, no matter how much hurt they
inflicted. Praying through the self-doubt and worry,

I let God comfort me and push away the darkness that wanted to consume me.

Continuing to meditate and focus on God and His Word, I fought away all the doubts and sadness on my ride to the diner.

Arriving at the curb at Dixie's, I paid the driver and got out. With the door to Dixie's in front of me, my heart began to pound. Flashing in my mind was Nathan when he stormed out of the diner just the other day over the pettiness of my speaking with Serenah about our struggles. Walking up to the door, I opened it while I prayed and walked in, entrusting the meeting with Nathan to God. *You showed me Your presence when I told him about the biopsy. Please, Lord, show me Your presence again.* Surveying the dining area inside, I saw Nathan across the restaurant in a booth that was near the back corner of the diner. My heart jumped into my throat and I almost cried on the spot, but I reined my emotions under control. *Help me, Lord,* I prayed as I walked in his direction. Nathan's eyes lifted and met mine. What felt like a million pieces of glass tore through my chest as he smiled at me. *How could he be smiling?* Then the smile fell into a grimace as I didn't return it.

Taking a seat, I said, "Hey."

"Hey." He seemed nervous as he fidgeted with his ring and then took a quick sip of the ice water in front of him. Placing it back on the napkin, he turned the cup and then brought his hands together in front of him. "I'm glad you decided to come." His words were heavy and dripped with sincerity. Part of me just wanted him to freak out so I could be done, but he didn't. He remained calm.

"What do you want to talk about, Nathan?" I finally asked.

"Let's talk about how this is going to work moving forward."

"It's not. I already told you it's over, from my point of view."

"Then why'd you come here then?" he pressed. Reaching his hand across the table, he attempted to grab mine, but I pulled it away.

"I wanted to hear you out, but it sounds like you have nothing to say. This was a mistake." I got up, but he grabbed my arm.

"No, wait. I do." The same server from the other night—Miley— came over to our table. I sat back down. She took our orders for dinner. Chicken fried steak for Nathan, while I elected to just have a cup of coffee. My appetite wasn't present. It hadn't been since he broke the news to me about the affair. As

the server left, Nathan looked at me again.

"Stop looking at me and just talk," I said.

"Otherwise, I'm just going to go."

"I want to make this work. Our marriage."

"Well, I don't," I replied bluntly as Miley returned

with my coffee. I smiled at her and thanked her. She

left the table again.

"Give me time to change your mind. One month."

"A month?" I asked.

"Yeah. A month. Then after that, if you still want a

divorce, go for it. I won't even contest it."

Furrowing my eyebrows at him, I said, "I don't know

about that, Nathan. What's your plan? To sweet talk

me and treat me nice for a month and think I'll just

magically love you again?"

"No," he replied, shaking his head. "Please. Give me

a month."

"You won't contest the divorce if I do this?" I asked as I contemplated his offer.

"Nope. I'll give you everything."

"Okay," I replied. "So what does that entail? What's first?"

"I'm coming back to the inn with you."

"No way. Not okay," I replied. "I can't lie next to you in bed."

"I'll sleep on the floor or even out on the balcony," he offered. His eyebrows were up, and he was serious.

I laughed at the mention of the outdoors. "The balcony?"

"Yeah."

"Okay. You sleep outside on that little balcony, and you can come back to the inn." While I didn't see our marriage coming back anytime soon, I did see some great entertainment coming my way. Knowing the low would be in the forties tonight, I felt a bit sinister in making him sleep out in the cold, but he deserved it. He lied for years, when I couldn't even keep in the fact of Derek for a day!

"Awesome. We have what, two days left at the inn?" he asked.

"Yeah. Serenah and I talked again. She knows you took off." *That was something that would drive him nuts,* I thought.

"That's good you have someone you can talk to."

Raising an eyebrow, I said, "Well, that's interesting, since you freaked out the other day about it."

"I was being selfish and prideful—both sins."

A burst of laughter erupted from my lips, and I quickly tried to cover my mouth. "I'm sorry," I said with a shrug. "I don't buy it, dude!"

"You don't have to buy it. I have a month to convince you I'm changed."

"Just because you're changed doesn't mean I can live with you the rest of my life, Nathan." The server returned to our table with his food, and he began to eat. My insides relaxed as there was some sort of plan to this chaos and an end in sight. We'd be okay in a month, or I'd be leaving in a month.

CHAPTER 7

After our meal at the diner, our daughter, Jenny,

called Nathan's phone. I had thought little of the

children since everything had happened. We found

a bench not far from the diner and sat. A little closer

than I preferred, but I wanted to make sure Jenny

could hear my voice. "How's it going with Grandma

and Grandpa?" I asked.

"It's good. Grandma showed us a bunch of photos of Dad when he was a baby . . ." She broke out into laughter. "You were such an ugly baby, Dad! That big head!"

Nathan let out a laugh. "Don't be mean! I turned into quite the stud!"

I flashed him an eye roll. Jenny went on to tell us about how she and Dakota took a hike up the hill on the property. They even made it to the top and found the tree Nathan had carved our names into when we were dating. The memory danced through my mind, and for a moment, I wasn't thinking about his betrayal.

"Did you guys make out up there?" Jenny pressed.

"Jennifer!" I said as I went red in embarrassment.

Nathan and I made eye contact for a moment, but I quickly broke away. We had more memories up on that hill than I could possibly try to count or would be appropriate for retelling to our daughter.

"Grandma said Daddy asked you to marry him up there."

My mind jumped back through time to the day. It hurt for the memory to come, knowing what I knew now, but I couldn't stop it.

We had been on a hike up to the top for a romantic picnic. We enjoyed those a lot in our youth since it was the only way we could be alone. That day, Nathan was in charge of packing the lunches and water bottles, but he forgot a very important thing— the lunch. After our bottles of water, he got down on a knee, and with a light breeze blowing in from the north, he asked me to marry him. He said if I said 'yes', that the event would make human history, for no other person alive could ever be made happier than him. The once-beautiful memory was now tainted with a vein of darkness. It pained me to relive it.

"What did you love most about Dad when you guys were dating?" Jenny asked.

Overwrought with emotional turmoil, I stood as my eyes watered and walked away from the bench. I needed to get away from that conversation. Stopping at a large iron horse randomly placed down the way from the bench, I peered up at the early evening sky. I looked at the clouds and prayed for God to give me strength and control over how I was feeling. Until this point, I hadn't thought about the impact of divorce on the kids. I was focused on myself and my own happiness. A part of me felt bad about that, but it was my marriage, not my children's. I knew I shouldn't stay with Nathan because of the kids, but they did weigh heavily on my mind in the moment.

Turning back toward the bench, I saw Nathan on

the phone with Jenny. He was smiling and laughing

like nothing was wrong. That was the right thing to

do though. It wasn't fair to bring them into the

middle of it right now.

A few moments later, Nathan hung up and walked

over to me. "You all right?"

I nodded.

"I had no idea that my mom would bust out the old

photo album."

"I know," I replied. "I love you too much to just walk

away from this marriage, Nathan, but I don't like

you right now. It's my love that made me say 'yes' to

a month, but I honestly don't think this can really

work out."

He grabbed my hands and looked into my eyes with

the same fear I had inside me. "I know. It seems unresolvable and there's so much pain. But we serve a God that does the impossible. Let's see what God can do before we get too drastic."

Tears streamed down my cheeks and I took a deep breath in. Letting it escape my lips, I replied, "Okay. We'll give it a try."

The fireplace back in the inn was roaring when we walked in the front door. Serenah called out from around the fireplace in the living room. "Is that you, Elizabeth?"

I glanced at Nathan, and he flashed me a curt nod in approval. We ventured into the living room to find Serenah and Charlie sitting on one of the couches.

He had one arm around her shoulders while he held a cup of iced tea in the other. They both smiled.

"Did you two want to join us?" Serenah asked.

Before I could say 'no', Nathan said, "Yes."

Raising an eyebrow, I looked at him. "Really?"

"Yeah. Why not?" Nathan replied as he walked over to the other couch in the room and took a seat.

Serenah hopped up and set her glass of iced tea down on the coffee table. "Let me get you guys something to drink. We have iced tea, water, and cola."

"Cola would be great," Nathan said. "I'm parched."

Serenah nodded and glanced over at me.

"Water for me," I replied, smiling as I joined Nathan on the couch. This was different and nice, but I knew Nathan was just trying to please me.

"Did you get the paddle boat repaired?" Nathan

asked, looking over at Charlie as Serenah went into the kitchen.

Finishing the last part of his cup of iced tea, Charlie set it down on a coaster beside him on an end table. "Yeah. It keeps leaking in this same spot, and I keep repairing it, but I think it's just going to need replaced."

"Oh, wow. How much do they run?" Nathan asked, crossing a leg over his knee.

"I could get one for about five hundred or so." Serenah returned with our drinks and smiled at me as she handed me my glass of water. She looked thrilled to see that Nathan had returned to the inn with me. I was happy too, but I was scared. I didn't trust him, and I had questions about the affair that I had to combat almost constantly.

"I see," Nathan replied to Charlie. "Think we might

try the canoe out again tomorrow—weather permitting, of course."

I laughed.

"That should be fun," Serenah said. "Oh, you know what? You guys should check out the walking path across the lake."

"Where at?" I asked.

"It loops up around that empty summer campground. The one with the buildings with green roofs. There's a really neat old church building back there, all dilapidated and whatnot." Serenah smiled over at Charlie. "That's where Charlie made his proposal to me. It was in the dead of winter and a little chilly, but the snow made for such a beautiful scene to remember the moment." She got up and went over into the other living room and grabbed a picture frame from a bookshelf. Walking back over, she showed it to me. "Isn't that gorgeous?"

"Really is," I replied as I smoothed my thumb over the glass. The shot was of Charlie on his knee and Serenah with her hand out. They were bundled up like a couple of Eskimos at the North Pole. "Who took the picture?"

"I brought a tripod in my backpack," Charlie said.

Nathan leaned over and looked. "Looks like fun. We'll have to check it out. We used to go on hikes and explore ruins all the time. Remember that trip to that one ghost town in Montana?"

I nodded. "We love history."

That evening, I saw Nathan talk, laugh and smile like I hadn't seen in a long time. His kindness and social skills shining didn't change the reality of what had happened. What he had done. What I had done. And though it didn't lessen the anger, hurt and pain

I felt inside, I knew God requires me to forgive. Not when convenient, not when it feels right, but to forgive. It wasn't about me and Nathan as much as it was between me and God. That reality set into me, and though it was hard to swallow, I knew I had to do it.

*

Waking in the middle of the night, I slipped out of bed to retrieve a bottle of water from the mini-fridge in the closet. After taking a drink, I lowered the bottle and could see out onto the balcony where Nathan was asleep. His feet were partially uncovered due to the small throw blanket covering him being too small. I felt bad. Seeing my own blanket from home plus the comforter on the bed in the room, I knew what I needed to do. Setting my water bottle down on the night stand, I took my blanket out to him and covered my husband up. He was sleeping like a rock even though it was cold outside. After covering him, I surveyed his face and his closed eyes. My heart felt a sting. Just looking at him hurt. *Why'd you have to do it, Nathan? Was it truly because of what I did to you? Was it revenge?* Though I had a million questions in my mind about his affair, I kept them to myself. I was scared to know the truths that lay between the details of his unfaithfulness. If thoughts had the power to kill, my imagination would have already killed me by now.

As I turned and went back inside, I heard Nathan wake up from the sound of the door opening. Looking over my shoulder at him, I saw his eyes glancing down at my blanket strewn across his midsection, and he smiled. "Thank you."

Stopping in the open door, I said, "You looked cold."

I went back inside. Before I could shut the door, he jumped up from under the covers and stopped the door from shutting. "What?"

"Can we talk?" he asked.

"It's like three in the morning, Nathan. We can talk tomorrow."

He shook his head and raised his eyebrows.

"Please?"

"Okay," I replied, letting loose the door so he could come in. We walked over to the bed and sat. He took my hand in his, but he wasn't saying anything. After a moment, I said, "Come on, Nathan. I'm falling asleep. Let's talk in the morning. I'm tired."

"Why haven't you asked any details about the affair? I know you kind of did, but you've drilled me with a slew of questions over a simple business convention before. I just expected more."

My heart felt like it skipped a beat. "Well, I haven't asked because I'm scared to know the details. I don't want that in my mind."

He nodded. "Okay."

"You do need to quit your job. You know . . . if we end up staying together—which I'm not saying is happening. You think you can really quit your job?"

"I'd do anything to keep you, Lizzy."

Though his words were dipped in tenderness and I could tell he was being truthful, I couldn't help but not to trust him. "Shouldn't have ever done it if you wanted to keep me so badly, Nathan."

"I'll quit my job right now." He pulled his cellphone out from his pocket and began texting. "I'm texting Alex right now to let him know I won't be back."

Panic gripped my core as I thought about all the income going out the window. I clung to his arm.

"How will we survive? Bills? Everything?"

He paused and looked at me. "We'll figure it out. God will provide." He took my hand and said, "Let's pray." We bowed our heads, and he led the prayer. "Heavenly Father, we come to You right now and give you this marriage and our finances. Help us not to worry in our time of need, but to trust You, God. For it is You who can heal this marriage, for it is You alone who knows the future and what will come of it. Please, Lord, comfort us. In Your Heavenly name we pray, Amen."

In the wee hours of the morning on that fifth day of June, I saw something I hadn't ever seen in my husband. A pure and undeniable faith in God. Sure, we went to church four years ago, but it was just the motions of doing the thing we thought was right.

This, though. This was real. He worked so hard to

get that job and get that career going, and he was

ready to toss it away. And he did just that—he quit.

CHAPTER 8

Rolling over in bed the next morning, I saw Nathan outside on the balcony. Behind the closed French doors, I could see he was on the phone and looked upset. My first thought was he was on the phone with Alex, then when I saw him wipe a tear from his eye, I thought the worst. *Was he talking to her? Did he never break it off?* My pulse raced as I quickly got out from the covers and went over to the door.

Opening it, I heard him ending the call.

"We'll be in touch," he said. Hanging up the phone, he turned and jumped a little. "Good morning."

"Startled?"

"Yeah, I didn't hear you come out . . ."

"You're up rather early." My eyes scanned him head to toe. A clean pair of shorts and a button up shirt were an easy indicator he had been up for a while.

"Alex called, so I needed to do some explaining to him. Then I just got in the shower and got ready." My eyes turned to his cellphone in his hand. "Then who were you talking to if you talked to Alex before the shower?"

"My father." He slipped his phone into his pocket and took a step closer. Touching my arms gently, he tilted his head as he gave me a soft look of genuine concern. "You okay?"

I let out a sigh as I shook my head. "I'm struggling with trusting you. I thought maybe it was that woman."

"No, I haven't talked to her since I broke it off. Look, I understand you're upset and not trusting me. It hasn't even been a day. It's going to take some time. Just tell me whatever you need, and I'll give it to you. Truly—anything."

My eyes trained on his shorts pocket that held his phone.

He pulled it out and handed it over to me. "Check it all out. I'm freely open to anything you need."

Glaring at him for a moment, I unlocked his phone and checked the call log. His story matched. *But he could have erased her from the log. Ugh!* Giving it back to him, I said, "I feel like an idiot. Checking your phone?" Pressing my hand against my forehead, I continued, "I get what I want and it's not even enough for my crazy mind! I feel like I could go through all your emails and pore over the phone bills, and I'd never be content with what I find."

He pressed his lips together to form a thin line as he put the phone back in his pocket. Giving me a nod, he sighed. "I'm sorry. It's my entire fault with what is going on in your head. It's going to be that way for a while, probably. You'll have to learn to trust me again. I've lost that right, and I get that."

A power tool fired up from beyond the balcony, coming from the direction of the shore. Looking past Nathan, I could see through the slats of wood and down to the grass near the shore. There was a group of guys and a pile of wood beside them.

Nathan glanced over his shoulder and said, "They're

building something down there. Not sure what.

Charlie was there a bit earlier and waved up at me."

"Hmm," I replied, walking past him and to the

railing. There were two men hauling wood down the

side of the house and down to the grass.

"We should get going on that canoe ride," Nathan

said, coming to my side. He touched my shoulder.

"All right," I replied. "Let me get ready." Turning

around, I went inside and to the bathroom. Nathan

stayed behind on the balcony.

After I got changed, I ran a brush through my hair in

the bathroom. As I stood in front of the mirror, I

smiled when I saw Nathan come through the door.

When he placed his hands on my hips, I felt a rush

of warmth come through me. I had forgotten the

affair, if only for a moment. Then, as his hands came

up my sides, I remembered. Tears started, and I

shifted out of his hands, turning away from him.

"Lizzy," he said gently.

"Sorry. I'm just not in the mood right now." I wiped my eyes and said, "I don't know what to do. This is so hard." My chin dipped to my chest.

He turned me around and lifted my chin with his finger. Looking into my eyes, he said, "I love you. I know it's hard. I hope I didn't make you uncomfortable with my touch."

I shook my head. "I want this to work. I really do. I just don't know how."

He nodded slowly as he pushed a strand of hair from my eyes and behind my ear. "We have to let God help us, Lizzy. It's going to take time, God, and probably some counseling too."

"Counseling? You refused to go—"

He raised a hand. "I know." He shook his head. "But

not anymore. When we get back to Spokane, we'll go. I promise."

"Thank you."

"We're only going to get better if we can focus on God and pray through the pain together. Can I pray with you right now?" he asked.

"Please," I said in a soft tone as I bowed my head.

"God," Nathan's voice was gentle as he continued, "We're two sinners who love You and want to honor You. We've messed up and come to You broken. We don't know what the future holds, but we know we *need* You. Help us, Lord. Amen."

"Amen," I replied, wiping my eyes.

Nathan dipped his chin, and a small smile broke from his lips. "I love you, Lizzy, and I'm so thankful you're trying to make this work with me. Don't mistake my smiles and joy for not acknowledging what's going on here. I just want to focus on the good while we work through this."

"You don't know how much that means to me," I replied. "I love you, Nathan."

Turning back around, I finished getting ready to leave for our trip across the lake. While this trip was becoming more transformative than I ever anticipated, I was thankful for whatever might come from it.

Walking through the abandoned summer campground that lay on the opposite side of the lake from *The Inn at the Lake*, Nathan and I searched for the path Serenah and Charlie had told us about. A few minutes into the overgrown grass, Nathan spotted an opening in the woods that ran alongside the camp ground.

Turning my steps, I followed beside him over to the path. As we entered the woods and onto the path, it narrowed. I fell behind while he led the way. Seeing him suddenly swat a bee from beside his face, I could almost feel the chills run down his spine. He was deathly allergic to the buzzing beauties of the air. When we were dating, he almost died from a bee sting. He even went into anaphylaxis, but his mother always had an EpiPen handy after a scare early in his childhood.

"Did you bring an EpiPen?" I asked.

"Yeah." He patted his cargo shorts' pocket. Relief came over me. I might have been angry, but I didn't want him to die.

Veering away from the campground, the path took

us up an incline. The farther we went, the steeper it became. Trees lined both sides, some dead while others not. Glints of the sunshine shone through the tops of the trees. Closer to the top of the hill, I saw a white weathered cross standing tall at the very top. I smiled. It looked battered but stood majestically tall. My exhaustion from the hike was made a bit more bearable as I kept my eyes fixed on the cross. Making it to the top, we found a boulder straightway and sat down. The burning sensation in my hamstrings eased as we both caught our breath.

"That's quite the hike!" I said as I caught my breath and wiped my brow from the sweat beading on my forehead.

Nathan used his shirt to wipe his face of sweat. He let out a big breath and said, "They failed to mention that part, didn't they?" Letting out a laugh, he stood up and walked. Peering down the incline we just came up, he said, "I bet that'd be fun to sled down."

Standing up, I replied, "Sure. Until you go off the path and hit a tree."

Turning around toward the path that continued, I could see the remains of the church house from the picture. Walking down the path, I came over to the structure. Overgrown grass mingled with broken shambles of the remains. My curiosity was piqued as I wondered how old the building was upon seeing green moss growing in crevices between the cracks on walls. A lone window sat in the front wall of the structure and was more of a rectangular hole than an actual window. Nathan walked up beside me and put his hand on the small of my back.

"Let's go check it out," he said, letting his hand fall away from my back and finding my hand. I was hesitant to hold his hand, but I allowed it. My impulse was to jerk away, but I knew that wouldn't help anything. As we walked, a summer breeze blew into the area, providing much-needed relief from the blazing heat of the sun.

Coming closer to the structure, our hands separated. Nathan went into the structure, and I brought my hand up to the outside wall. Touching the area between the window and the doorway, I let my fingers feel the grooves and texture. The uneven clay and rock was weathered and easily told of coming from a different time. "I wonder what this church's story is," I said as I let my fingers slide down and away from the wall.

Nathan climbed over rubble inside the building and over to a wide spot of light shining down through the opening in the roof. Peering up through the hole, he said, "This place is so old."

"What's that?" I asked, pointing to something I could barely make out in the corner of the room. Nathan looked over. Carefully, he stepped over more rubble and made his way over to the corner of the structure. Quickly looking at the ceiling inside, I came to the determination it would not fall on him, and that brought me comfort.

Watching Nathan, I saw him bend down in the corner. He tried to dislodge the object but it appeared stuck beneath a slab of broken clay and rock that looked to be part of the roof. "It's a box. Come help, Lizzy."

Hurrying over to him, I got down on my hands and knees and grabbed at the box as he tried to lift the slab of rock and clay. "Almost . . ." I said as I yanked. Letting out an unintelligible grunt, Nathan forced the slab up just a little more. It was enough for me

to pull it out. Just as I retrieved it, he released,

letting the rock and clay come crashing down on the

rest of the rubble, causing a plume of dust to push

up into the air.

The mangled metal box was gray with hints of rust

all over it. I smoothed my thumb over the dented

top and arrived at a lock. I jerked on it, but it was

too strong. I handed the box to Nathan as he came

up to me.

With the box in hand, he went over to a piece of

rock nearby and smashed the container against it.

Then again. The third swing worked, and the lock

broke away. Stepping over to him as he rose to his

feet, we both looked as he opened the lid.

An old yellow-tinted picture was inside. There was a

man and woman with a few kids standing outside

the church. Peering out through the doorway, I could see the spot they would have stood. Pulling it out of the box, I flipped it over and saw a date—1904.

"Look at this," Nathan said, pulling out a burnt newspaper clipping from the box a moment later. Squinting as I came in for a closer look at the clipping, I pulled Nathan's hand up to my face. There was a partial view of the woman's face. "That's the same lady from the picture."

Nathan peered around the remains of the building and said, "Maybe we can dig something up on this building in town? Like, some kind of historical documents?"

"Maybe," I replied as I looked at the picture again in my hand.

Placing the picture and clipping back into the box,

we headed out of the ruins and started back on the path toward our canoe. As we were walking down the steep hill that led back to the campground, Nathan asked, "You think a bomb hit the building to do that?"

I laughed as I peered back up at him behind me. "I seriously doubt that."

"What could make that massive hole in the ceiling like that?" He shook his head. "Just weird."

"I'm not sure," I replied. "Maybe we'll find out more in Newport."

CHAPTER 9

Arriving back across the lake to the inn, we saw

Charlie speaking with the construction workers in

the grass by the shore. My curiosity, along with my

attention, was focused on the newspaper clipping

and discovering the history behind the church more

than anything else. That wasn't the case for Nathan.

"Hey, Charlie," Nathan said as we pulled the canoe

up into the grass. He walked through the grass over to Charlie.

Charlie turned and came over to him. "Hey."

"What are they building?" Nathan asked, looking past him to the men who were now working on framing the base of some structure.

"A gazebo. It's for our wedding coming up next month. Serenah always saw one in her dreams as a teenager when she thought of her wedding day. I want to give her that." He smiled as he looked at the men. "I would have built it myself, but I'm so slammed at work that I barely have any time."

Work. The word off his lips jolted me out of my focus on the history of the church building. *Work. Nathan. The affair.* Within a mere second, I was almost in tears. All the truths of what had happened came rushing back at once. "I have to use the restroom," I said quickly. Heading up to the inn with the box, my tears wouldn't listen to my pleas of stopping the water works. Quietly, I cried on my way up the steps to the main level balcony.

Getting to the top, with the doorway in sight, I hurried my steps across the balcony. Turning the corner, Serenah came outside. "Elizabeth, are you all right?" she asked. Looking past her, I could see the bathroom door that would have been my safety away from the world if she hadn't stopped me.

I lost it.

Shaking my head, I began to cry and glanced over my shoulder toward the water. "No. I'm not. Everything was fine, and then boom . . . it wasn't. I don't know how to deal with this."

"Can we pray about it?" she offered, tilting her head slightly as she came over to me and touched my arm. When I looked up at her, I didn't see judgment in her eyes—but compassion. She cared. Giving her a nod, we bowed our heads and she prayed. "God. We come to You asking for help. Help for Elizabeth during this time of suffering. Help her to lean on You and the promises You make. Help her to feel Your comfort and let Your love consume her like a fire. We pray in Your name, Amen."

My nerves relaxed, and my breathing returned to normal shortly thereafter. "Thank you."

"You're welcome. Take a seat, and I'll get you a glass of water. You look parched." Serenah turned around and went inside.

"Thanks," I replied as I sat down in a chair outside on the balcony. A breeze lightly blew through the air and brought more relaxation to my body and soul. I peered across the lake. Stunned by the beauty in the moment, I shook my head in disbelief. *God is so big, so in control of everything, yet I still freak out.*

Coming back outside, Serenah handed me a glass of water and sat down in a chair beside me. Looking over at me, she said, "I'm sorry your time here has been such a struggle."

"Oh, it's not your fault, Serenah. I'm sorry I've made my personal life your problem."

She shook her head and smiled at me. "Don't be silly. I love helping people, and praying is a great way to tap into the source of the Almighty God."

"I just don't get why life has to be so hard sometimes," I said, letting out a sigh right before taking a drink of my water. "I don't see how or why God would let difficulties and trouble fall on good people."

"God didn't author sin, Elizabeth. The fall of

humanity was by our own choice to disobey God—

well, Adam and Eve. Most problems in our life come

down to a problem of the heart and selfishness. God

never once says our life will be easy in the Bible, but

He does tell us over and over again to trust in Him

and not to be afraid."

"But there's no purpose in the pain," I replied.

"That's not true," she replied. "Our relationship with

God can grow our faith through the difficult times.

We have to put our trust in Him, and when we do

that, amazing things can and *do* happen. I

remember when I left my abusive husband—I was

terrified. The future was so unclear and chaotic, but

the Lord provided, like He always does. Not in our

timing, but in His timing." Serenah sat up in her seat

and leaned, pointing toward the dividing line

between the properties where a bunch of trees were.

"There's a tree in there."

Recalling the small tree in the midst of the dirt I saw

the other day, I said, "I saw it. Smaller, right?"

"Yep. That tree is a memorial for my baby girl whom

I miscarried. It also serves as a reminder to me of

where I came from. My past. God delivered me and

set me free." She looked at me and reached a hand

over, placing it atop mine. "God will get you through

this storm. We can't merely just say we trust in God.

We have to put *our* trust in God."

"Are you saying I need to stay with my husband after

he cheated?" I asked, perplexed.

"No. I didn't say that. I left John, girl. You do what

you have to do. What I'm saying is to trust God no

matter what happens and whatever the outcome is."

I nodded and looked down at Nathan in the grass by

the shore. He was now laughing with Charlie about

something, and I smiled. Nathan was a good man with a good heart. He made a mistake, just like I did.

"What's the box about?" Serenah asked, breaking my thoughts.

Turning to her, I opened it and let her look inside. "We found it in the old church underneath the rubble."

"Oh, cool! Isn't that church neat?" she asked.

"It really is," I replied. Showing her the photo and newspaper clippings, I watched her reaction as her eyes widened. She was just as excited as Nathan and I were. She recommended we venture over to the library. According to Serenah, the library kept copies of all the old newspapers from Newport and surrounding areas.

Arriving at the library after grabbing a bite at Steve's Pizzeria, Nathan held open the door and gave a little bow as I walked in. A smile slipped onto my lips as I recalled how he used to do that same thing all the time when we were younger. He did a lot of things when we were younger that had fallen to the wayside.

Once inside, we found our way to a counter with a librarian behind it. "Where do you keep the old newspaper clippings?" Nathan asked. "We're trying to find a—"

"That way," the librarian replied curtly, pointing without letting him finish. Her finger extended over to a row of computers that sat against a wall, parallel to a bookcase. "Those computers have digital copies of all the newspapers dating back to the foundation of the town."

"Thank you," Nathan replied.

He placed his hand on the lower part of my back for a moment, and we turned and headed over to the computers. We each took a computer and sat down side-by-side. We began searching through the digital archives of newspaper clippings.

After a few minutes of browsing aimlessly on both our accounts, Nathan said, "I'm backing up to 1900 and starting there." Adjusting in his seat as he narrowed his look on the screen, he looked like he did back in college—focused. It stirred a younger part of my old self I hadn't been acquainted with in almost two decades. Those days back in college, right after we were married, we had the most passion filled nights ever, often not ending until the next morning.

"I'll start with 1902 and work my way up," I replied.

Minutes soon turned into hours, and hope of finding anything useful dwindled. Then it happened. While resting my face against my hand as I tried holding my head up, I saw the woman's face.

I let out a cheerful glee as I jumped.

"Quiet," Nathan said playfully as he scooted his chair over. Leaning forward, he placed his arm gently behind my back, barely letting his skin press against my back as he read the computer screen aloud.

"William and Mary Johnson founded the Sunnyside Chapel in the summer of 1903 in the hopes of providing a place of worship to the residents of Diamond Lake who live on the northern side of the lake. William had hopes to build a full-sized church, but he was unable to come up with the needed funds to do so. Services are on Sunday mornings at nine am and eleven thirty am." Relaxing back in his chair, Nathan raised his eyebrows and looked over at me. "That's pretty neat."

I nodded and pulled out the picture in my pocket. Smoothing my thumb over the picture, I was happy to have names to the faces.

"Look," Nathan said. Peering up at the screen, I saw he had clicked through more clippings and found another article about the chapel.

Setting the picture down on the desk, I leaned forward and read aloud. "Sunnyside Chapel on Friday, December 13, 1904. Just six months after opening its doors, Sunnyside Chapel has been closed due to inclement weather. A tree fell onto the chapel, causing part of the roof to collapse. The owners, William and Mary Johnson, are unable to finance the repairs at this time and have been forced to close the doors until the funds are raised. A joint service will be held at ten am in their home at 2482 Lancaster Road."

"Sad . . ." Nathan said. "They barely got started, and that happened?"

I nodded. "They never got the funds."

We continued searching for another hour, but the librarian soon came over to us and gave us the boot at five o'clock. We were both feeling a bit hungry, so we headed over to Dixie's diner to regroup our thoughts and discuss using our last day at the inn to visit the library once more.

After finishing our club sandwiches, we sat and spoke of what years to research the next day.

"What about 1905?" I asked as Miley refilled my water.

She raised a curious eyebrow at me, so I told her

what was going on.

"That sounds like fun. I bet Donald Atkins might know a thing or two. His family is one of the founders of Newport back in the late 1800s."

Nathan agreed with a nod. "We saw that name come up a ton in the old newspaper clippings. Where can we find him?"

"He likes to come in for coffee in the mornings. Try to be here around eight." Miley left our table and went to the next table. My eyes turned to Nathan. Smiling, I asked, "Wanna talk to this Atkins guy?"

Reaching across the table, his hand touched mine. He returned my smile and said, "Yeah. Sounds like fun."

Though I was loving his touches all day, my worry soared. *What if he hurts me again?* The 'what if's' were going to drive me nuts if I focused on them.

Doing what Serenah recommended, I focused on the good.

CHAPTER 10

In our room back at the inn, Nathan drew a bath in

the Jacuzzi. Tossing in some lavender bath salts, he

glanced over at me. "I promise to keep my shorts

on," he said with a raised brow. The trouble with

that was I knew Nathan more than he realized.

"I don't think a dip in the Jacuzzi would be a good

idea," I replied, smiling. Going over to the duffel bag

in the room, I grabbed my book and headed toward the balcony. Flipping on the light switch just inside the door, I turned on the light outside and went out. Relaxing into a chair outside, I began to read.

Not more than a minute passed before Nathan opened the door. Turning, I looked back and up at him. He smiled and came out in nothing but his trunks. Walking over to me, he bent down and looked me in the eyes. Letting the back of his fingers gently glide against my arm, he said, "Please join me in the Jacuzzi. We can't leave this place without you at least trying it out."

Smiling out of the corner of my mouth, I closed my book and looked at him. "How can I trust you in a Jacuzzi? I know you, Nathan."

He smiled, letting his head drop. Then he looked at me again. "Look at it like a trust building exercise. I promise to not do anything you don't want." He took my free hand in both of his and kissed my open palm. "Trust me."

"Okay," I replied. Taking my book, I followed him inside and tossed it on the bed. Nathan climbed in the Jacuzzi while I went into the bathroom. After I slipped into my one-piece swimming suit, I looked into the mirror. I looked happy. *Today was a good day,* I thought to myself.

Exiting the bathroom, I came over to the Jacuzzi and climbed in. Nathan eyeballed me as I got in the opposite end from him. I shot him a suspicious glare.

"My shorts are on," he said with a laugh in his voice. As I lowered myself into the Jacuzzi, bubbling hot water wrapped itself around me as the smell of lavender filled my nose. My tight muscles from the day suddenly began to loosen, and every part of my arms, back and legs fell into a deep relaxation. "This is amazing," I said as I closed my eyes.

"I know," he replied.

"Why don't you turn on the game?" I asked as I opened my eyes and looked at him.

He shook his head. "I don't care about the game."

There was truth in his words. I could sense it. He really was a changed man from the one I showed up with to the inn. "I'm curious. Why the sudden and quick changes, Nathan?"

Looking away from me, he said, "Honestly? The biopsy. It woke me up. No longer was it just about my being unhappy or some stupid, petty thing like fighting. You could have had cancer. Could have died. The truth is, Lizzy, I love you. I was being selfish, and I was in the wrong."

"I see . . ."

"Yeah," he said gently. "I was being stupid and giving in to my flesh. It wasn't right. I'm so sorry, Lizzy. I'm going to spend my entire life making it up to you. You deserve better than me, and if you do stay with me, I'm going to do my best to make you happy every day. God willing, and with His help, of course."

His words tipped me over the edge in a good way. Between his subtle touches and now the outpouring of love from his lips, I was overwhelmed with the warmth of his love. Sitting up in the Jacuzzi, I brought a finger up and motioned him to come closer. He smiled and adjusted his legs under the water to be around mine. He shook his head and smiled. Pulling me by the arms gently, he brought me into his arms. Only a few inches were between us. Looking into my eyes, he tilted his head and brought a hand up. Gently brushing my cheek, he said, "You truly are the most beautiful woman on earth." He leaned in and let his lips gently press against mine.

My heart fluttered as my mind cleared of any thought. Kissing him back, I let the warmth of our love flow through my body. Grabbing onto my shoulders, he pulled me closer to him. Wrapping my arms around his neck as his lips traveled from my mouth down my neck, I felt more connected to him than I had in years.

CHAPTER 11

Rolling over the next day, I looked at Nathan as he was still asleep next to me. Smiling, I framed his face with a hand. Last night had been amazing. Blinking his eyes open, he grinned up at me.

"Morning, beautiful."

"Good morning," I replied.

Nathan asked, "How are you?"

Furrowing my eyebrow at him, I asked, "What do you mean?"

"Your heart." His eyebrows went up. "How are you feeling?"

"I'm okay," I replied confidently as I nodded.

We got out of bed and headed downstairs for breakfast with Serenah. As we talked with her, my mind soon wandered back to Nathan's affair. I wanted to forget about it and just never look back, but I couldn't. Not finishing my breakfast, I took the remainder of my eggs and toast and threw them away in the kitchen.

On the way into Newport, Nathan picked up on my uneasiness in the car and asked, "What's wrong, Lizzy?"

Shaking my head, I looked away and out my window as tears welled in my eyes. He tried touching my shoulder, but I rolled out of it. With a shaky voice, I said, "I can't just . . . just shake what happened. I want to move on *so* badly. I do. I just don't know how."

He was silent.

"You didn't just cheat on me once, Nathan. There were multiple times. Do you know how much that hurts me? I felt like complete garbage for years about what I did three years ago. Yet you had seen someone else in a very intimate way for a month."

"Oh . . ." he replied softly.

Reaching over, I touched his hand and said, "I know I'm sending mixed signals. Yesterday was amazing with the church and the history thing we're trying to figure out, but . . ." I shrugged. "It's just a distraction from the reality." Tears ran down my cheeks.

"Tomorrow, we're going home, and then . . . I don't

know, Nathan. I just don't know what's going to happen."

Wiping a tear from his eyes, he turned and said, "I won't make you wait a whole month. I won't fight it even if you want to go file when we get home. What I did was horrid."

We pulled into the diner just then, and he parked the car. Turning to him, I said, "I appreciate that. I don't know what I'll ultimately do at this point, but know that I'm trying."

He nodded and wiped his eyes of more tears.

Getting out of the car, we went inside the diner and sat in a booth. Glancing around the diner, there were a few different older men sitting and drinking coffee.

Nathan leaned across the table and said, "Wonder which one is him."

A waitress arrived to our table. "Hi, I'm Charlotte. I'm new here. New in the sense I haven't worked here before." Her voice quieted as she turned red. "I didn't need to say that . . ." She glanced back at the waitress watching her. Turning back to us, she continued, "Anyway, what can I get you guys to eat? I mean . . . drink?"

"Coffee," Nathan and I both said at the same time. We looked at each other and smiled as we lightly laughed. Though the conversation in the car was difficult, it didn't keep us from being able to enjoy the cuteness of what had just happened.

"That's cute. You two are cute together," Charlotte replied. "I'll be back with that, and that should give you some time to decide on breakfast."

"Wait," Nathan said. She paused and turned back to us as he continued, "We're not going to eat. Can you help us with something else?"

Her eyebrows shot up. "What's that?"

I smiled at her and said, "We're trying to get some history on Newport."

"I grew up here and have pretty close ties to the Townsons, one of the early families that first settled here. What are you after?"

"Really?" I replied. "We were coming in to speak with Donald Atkins." The name caused her to grimace. "We're after information on an old family called the Johnsons. That name mean anything to you? They had a little chapel on the north side of Diamond Lake back in the early 1900s."

"I'm sorry. I don't know anything about that." She gave a curt nod to one of the nearby tables. "*Donald* is that guy over there with silver hair."

We both glanced over and looked at him. "Thanks,"

I said. Charlotte and the other server behind her left our table soon after.

Nathan and I both got out of the booth. Looking at Nathan, I asked, "You know what you're going to say?"

"Just going to ask about the family," he replied. Glancing over at him, he asked, "Was there something different I should ask that I'm not aware of?"

I shook my head. "No. That's a good plan." Looking over at Donald, I saw that *Old Man Grump* look on his face. I turned back to Nathan. "You go. I'm going to stay. He doesn't look like the type of guy you want to ambush."

"Okay." Nathan tenderly kissed my cheek and then went over to the man's table. I sat back down in the booth. Raising my hand to my face, I touched my cheek where he had kissed me. *He's so sweet.* My eyes became watery. *Stop being so emotional!* I told myself. After a few minutes went by and Nathan was still over at the table talking to him, I peered over at them to see how it was going.

"Here's your coffee," Charlotte said, setting our coffees down on the table.

"Thank you," I replied, turning my attention to the cups.

As she left the table, Nathan came back over to the table and sat down. He had a grin from ear to ear on his face.

"Out with it!" I insisted with a smile.

Taking a sip of his coffee, he set it down and said, "Okay." His eyes floated back over toward the direction of Donald and then back at me. "I got a bit more information than I asked for, but it was interesting for sure. As for the Johnsons, William and Mary were the community's go-to people for all matters of the faith—kind of neat." Nathan took another sip of his coffee before continuing. "Donald also said the two of them were unable to have children, so they kind of took the whole community under their wing, instructing and solving most disputes around the lake and in Newport. Donald made a point to say it was highly unusual for a woman to have that kind of role in the early 1900s, but Mary was regarded as a virtuous woman and respected community-wide." He leaned across the table and said, "It gets dark though."

Raising an eyebrow in curiosity as I leaned in, I asked, "How?"

He looked hesitant to continue.

"Come on, Nathan. Just tell me."

"William beat Mary on several occasions. Really badly. This Donald guy's family kept journals dating back to the foundation of the town. The diaries talk about how Mary would come over with multiple cuts and bruises across her face and all over her body. Donald's great-great-grandmother, who wrote the journal, was a nurse. She'd help clean the wounds and bandage her up."

Shaking my head, I felt a sting in my heart for Mary. "How on earth? They worked for Christ and did His work. How could that kind of thing go on?"

Nathan said, "Donald told me that kind of thing was common back then, but the real truth was that Mary cared more about the Lord. Elle, the great-great-grandmother, tried to tell her to leave him, but she wasn't concerned about her husband's misdealings with her. Instead, her desire was to care for the townspeople."

"That's messed up," I said.

"Yeah, it is. That period was a lot different from today though. It's really hard to swallow. No woman should ever go through something like that." Nathan shook his head with a look of disgust. "Not right."

I nodded.

"Oh, something weird I learned. Kind of explains that sideways look Charlotte gave us when we mentioned the Atkinses."

Leaning in, I raised my eyebrows, "Do tell!"

"The Townsons and the Atkins family have been feuding since the foundation of this town. Something about a golden bell in the lake?"

"Wow," I replied. "Why?"

"Donald said the town was transporting a large golden bell across the lake that the Atkins paid for when a storm blew in and the boat sank. The bell was supposed to be where that large iron horse is in the center of town."

"Intriguing," I replied.

"I know, right?" Nathan replied. "I guess the other family, the Townsons, claim *they* were the ones who paid for it and it belongs to them."

"Doesn't it belong to the town?" I asked.

He shook his head. "No. After not being able to recover the bell, the town decided to withdraw their interest in it."

"Odd," I replied. "Couldn't someone just use equipment to find it?"

"It's forbidden on the lake. That's why it's so peaceful."

Donald Atkins walked by just then and tipped his chin to Nathan on his way out of the diner. Looking past him, I could see Charlotte shoot an ice cold glare in Donald's direction. "Charlotte just glared at Donald. This feud is really still going on after all these years?"

Nathan peered over his shoulder toward the waitress and nodded. "Very much so. Donald seemed angry to merely speak about the Townsons." Turning his eyes back to me, Nathan reached across the table and grabbed onto both my hands. "I miss you, Elizabeth. I miss this. Us being us. Together. Enjoying life."

Though it pained me on levels I couldn't even fully comprehend, I couldn't help but agree with a smile on my face and joy in my heart. "I miss us, too."

Tomorrow morning lingered in the back of my mind as I looked at him. We'd be heading back to reality. Nathan had no job, and we had a mortgage payment due in a few weeks. Though we had enough savings to last us for a couple of months, it wasn't ideal to dig into that. The thought of returning home was a bit unnerving to me and caused my stomach to turn and my blood pressure to rise just thinking about it.

For dinner that final evening, Nathan offered to run to Newport and pick something up for us while I stayed back and packed our bags. I agreed. As I walked the room and retrieved dirty clothing, I stopped near the window. The lake still captivated me just as it did the first time I saw it when we arrived. Seeing an eagle fly from a branch, I watched. It swooped down to the water and glided across the surface of the water, then shot upward into the sky.

Freedom, I thought to myself as I watched the eagle fly into the distance. *I could be free. Free from pain and heartache.* All I had to do was file for divorce. My mind lingered over to Mary Johnson. It bothered me to know she was physically battered by her husband and stayed with him. I was no Mary. Though I hadn't suffered from physical beatings, I had enough emotional scarring to last a lifetime. *It's not wrong to leave him,* I told myself. *What's the right thing to do?* I prayed in the moment.

As I was finishing up with packing, a knock came at the door. "Come in," I said as I placed my flip-flops into the duffel bag.

"Hey," Serenah said gently. "You'll be gone tomorrow, and I wanted to give you a verse to meditate on as you find yourself back in the realities of daily life."

Raising an eyebrow, I said, "Oh, yeah? What verse?"

"First Peter 5:7. It's not something I do with all my guests, but I feel like you and I . . ."

"Connected?" I offered, finishing her sentence.

She broke out in a smile as she came closer. She grasped onto my arms and said, "Yes! I had a really nice time talking to you."

I let out a sarcastic laugh. "Listening to my drama, you mean."

"No. Not at all," she replied. Her eyes surveyed the room and looked over to the window I had been standing at earlier. "You're going to be okay, Elizabeth."

Letting out a relieved sigh, I said, "Thanks. You don't know how much I needed to hear that right now."

She looked at me. "What would you like for your final breakfast? How does a sausage, egg and cheese muffin sandwich sound?"

"Delicious." Zipping the zipper on the duffel bag, I let my hands fall to my sides. "Done." I turned to her. "Thank you for listening to me and praying with me. I appreciate it all more than words can tell."

Serenah placed a hand on my shoulder and said, "You're welcome." She pointed to the nightstand on Nathan's side. "There's a notebook in there if you want to leave a note for future guests." She gave me a hug and left the room.

Sitting down on the edge of the bed on Nathan's side, I pulled out my phone and went to the Bible app to look up the verse.

Cast all your anxiety on him because he cares for you.

1 Peter 5:7

After reading the verse, I closed my phone and opened the drawer. A little blue notebook along with a pen sat at the bottom of the drawer. Pulling it out, I opened it up and scanned the pages. Stories of anniversaries and newly-weds filled most of the pages, and then I came to a blank page. This page was mine. Smoothing out the page, I placed the date up in the corner and then began to write.

CHAPTER 12

After a delightful breakfast the next morning, it was
time to go back home. After exchanging goodbyes
with Charlie and Serenah, Nathan and I got in our
car and headed to Moses Lake. Our kids, Jenny and
Dakota, were already eagerly awaiting our arrival.
Two and half hours was a long time in the car with
anyone, let alone with a betraying spouse. The quiet

wasn't good in the car. It allowed my mind to think, to wander and linger in areas I didn't want it to go. Places I had been able to avoid for the most part.

I made it to the one-hour mark.

Silent tears streamed down my cheeks, giving away the storm of emotions raging inside.

Nathan noticed.

"Lizzy?" he asked gently.

Wiping my eyes, I asked, "What?"

"You're crying. What's wrong?" Reaching a hand over, he placed it on top of my hand that rested on my thigh.

"Really?" I snapped, pulling my hand away. I crossed my arms and looked out the window. "I'm sorry. I just feel so anxious. I can't control my thoughts, my emotions. It hurts."

"Say what you need to say. I can handle it, Lizzy. Tell

me what's going on inside that heart of yours." He adjusted in his seat. "You deserve to express it to me."

"You made me feel unloved," I replied, keeping my eyes on the blur of scenery outside my window. "Right now, I feel dirty knowing that you were sleeping with her. The thought *literally* makes me feel like vomiting." I began crying. "I'm not trying to be mean right now. I'm just scared and confused—which probably seems weird after the other night."

"I know it does little to ease the pain, but I'm sorry." He looked over at me with tears running down his cheeks. "Sleeping out on that balcony was tough. Not because it was super cold—which it was—but because every time I woke up in the middle of night, I saw you through the doors, and it killed me all over again for what I had done to us. I feel like a piece of trash for what I've done to you, and I wouldn't blame you if you left me when we got home. I fully expect it."

"How'd you cheat on me without any difficulties? Any struggle? For an entire month? How could you look me in the eye daily and feel no remorse for your own affair? How could you not even feel bad?" I asked as tears streamed down my cheeks and my heart spilled out.

He shook his head. "You think I didn't feel bad? Or feel any remorse? I can't count how many sleepless nights I had debating on telling you. I came so close so many times. It's fine for you to be angry. It's fine if you want to end our marriage, but don't sit there and tell me I didn't struggle with this." More tears came as his defenses lowered and he continued, "I don't understand how I, who call myself a man of

God, could screw up so badly."

My mind jumped back to the Johnsons and how William beat his poor wife. "Humanity is ugly. It's not pretty. It's in a fallen state. If you find ten righteous in that city, would you spare the whole city? Remember that with Abraham talking to God?" Nathan nodded slowly, and tears continued down his cheeks. "We need God," he replied. "All of us. It's not just a saying we sing in a song or post on Facebook. It's a way of life. Or at least, that's what it's supposed to be." Wiping his eyes, he took a deep breath in and let it out. "I've never prayed as much as I've prayed these last few days at the inn." He looked over at me as he continued, "Even though I went to church my whole life and read the Bible a couple of times over, it was always just part of my life. In a box of its own almost. The problem with that is it wasn't my entire life—just part. A cute little box that I pulled out when convenient."

"What are we going to do?" I asked, looking to Nathan for hope.

"Well, we're going to go to counseling," he said gently as he reached over and grabbed onto my hand. "We don't need to tell the kids anything about what's going on."

"Okay. I agree."

"Does that mean you aren't divorcing me?" he asked.

"I'm not making promises, Nathan. Let's start with counseling."

Walking through the front door of our house filled me both with a feeling of relief to finally be home and a sense of uncertainty for the coming days.

Jenny and Dakota promptly ran up to their rooms.

Surveying the living room as I walked in, I felt like

the entire house was from a different part of my life.

The life in which I was ignorant of the truth. A time

in which I did everything to get closer to a man who

was secretly seeing someone else. Seeing the brown

sofa in the living room, I thought about the nights

crying into the armrest, waiting for him to come

home. Worried he left me because of what I had

done three years ago. My eyes welling with tears, I

hurried through the living room and into the

bathroom.

Locking the door behind me, I flipped on the light

and gripped both sides of the sink tightly. The

mirror showed me a reflection I didn't recognize.

Someone changed. I saw a deep hurt behind those

sad blue eyes of mine. The scars I had brought home with me were deeper than I could have ever imagined. *How am I ever to live in this house, God?*

A light knock came on the door. Turning, I feared it was Nathan. "I'm kind of busy."

"Oh. Sorry, Mom," Dakota replied. Hearing him walk away, I felt bad.

Turning my eyes back to the mirror, I gave myself a pep talk. "You are a mother. You are a wife. You are a beautiful person. If you cannot handle being with Nathan, you will leave. It's Biblical to leave. You have the power to decide." It did little to help, but it did encourage me.

Walking out of the bathroom, I saw Nathan sitting on the couch with a picture frame in hand. He smoothed his thumb over the glass as I walked over and sat down beside him. With tear-filled eyes, he looked at me and said, "I jeopardized everything important to me. My whole life." He set the picture down and wrung his hands. Looking around the room, his eyes fell on the picture of dogs playing poker on the wall near the television. He said, "That picture you hate is coming down."

"Why?" I asked as he got up and walked over to the wall.

Taking it down, he looked back at me and said, "I'll show you. I'll be back in a bit." He took off out the front door with the keys to his car and left.

Pulling out my phone, I called the one person who knew what was going on—Serenah. When she answered, I almost hung up.

"Hello?" she said a second time.

"Hey. It's me, Elizabeth."

"Oh, hey. How are things going?"

"I'm sorry I called," I said as I stood and went into the kitchen. "I shouldn't—"

"No, no. It's fine, dear. What's going on?" she asked.

Plugging in the coffee pot, I replied, "This is harder than I thought. Everything in this house is a reminder."

"Did you read that verse? Treat it like an affirmation and memorize it. Every time you start to feel that anxiety rising in you, just repeat the verse out loud a couple of times." I was quiet without a response as I went back to the living room to retrieve my Bible.

"You know, Elizabeth. If you can't do it, it's okay. Biblically, you can divorce Nathan for what he did. There's no rule against it."

"I know. My mind says cut the jerk loose, but my heart and soul say to *try*. He really seems changed, but it's my own mind that is the problem." Opening up my Bible, I continued, "I'll work on that verse. Take care."

"Oh, wait. I need your address. For the wedding invitation. I want to get those sent out in the coming week."

After giving her my address, we hung up.

Highlighting 1 Peter 5:7 wasn't enough. I used the white space beside the text to make a drawing. The image I drew were the hands of the Lord holding the whole world. In the world I wrote the words: hate, worry, anxiety, and fear. I did this because God was my redeemer and I needed to commit to Him everything. Truly everything.

After an hour passed, Nathan returned home with a

wooden-framed picture of some sort. "Went to Kinko's," he said, shutting the door behind him. "But then I figured out they didn't have a frame and it'd be kind of lame without one . . . so I had to go hunting for one around town. I hope I didn't worry you."

Watching from the couch as he went over to the wall, I said, "No. I wasn't worried. What is the picture?"

"You'll see in just a second," he replied as he leaned the framed picture against the wall. "Kids, come downstairs, please," he hollered toward the direction of the stairs.

"I found us an appointment," I said. "It's for the day after tomorrow at two o'clock at Pines Baptist."

"Okay. Good."

Soon, Jenny and Dakota came downstairs to join us

in the living room.

"Sit by your mother, kids," Nathan requested as he pointed to the couch. As they walked over, he continued, "I know we haven't had the best church attendance the last little while."

"Try forever," Jenny replied with a laugh as she sat on the couch.

"Watch it," Nathan warned. "It's been about four years, but that's going to change." He turned and picked up the framed picture and hung it up. In beautiful cursive baby-blue handwriting, it read . . . *as for me and my household, we will serve the Lord. Joshua 24:15.*

"I love it," I said.

Nathan nodded and glanced at it for a moment and then turned to the kids. "Our house is going to revolve around this verse. We won't just go to church on Sundays. We will live the testimony of Christ and serve Him in this house. Sitting in your room all day? No. Try one or two hours, and the rest of the time down here as a family. Also, there will be family time in which we read Scripture and study. When we invest our time into something, that's where our heart is." He pointed to the verse. "Our hearts are going to abide in the Lord."

"What?" Jenny replied, annoyed. "You can't force God on us like this, Dad. That's not fair! We're Christians and have been baptized. You don't need to drill it into us more than that. I have a life."

"You're two years away from graduating. You deal with the rules until then, and *then* if you don't like them, you can leave."

"This isn't fair," Jenny said as she rose to her feet.

"Not another word about it. We'll talk more once

your mother and I come up with a solid plan. For now, you two can go back to what you were doing." After the kids were back in their rooms and I heard the doors shut, I patted the seat beside me on the couch. "What has gotten into you?" I asked as he sat down.

"Something on the trip to my parents' house really clicked for me today. After we talked about Abraham, I began thinking about other people in the Bible, and I realized a ton of them were messed up." He laughed and shook his head. "It's actually sad, not funny, but anyway, I thought about David. He messed up big time with Bathsheba, but he was still considered a man after God's own heart. It was his faith and reliance on the Lord that kept David in the long run." Nathan's eyes returned to the verse on the wall. "God's the only way this family can heal.

It's the only true way to do life." Turning back to me again, he placed his hand on top of mine. "It's how *we* can heal."

While I didn't trust Nathan fully, I trusted the Lord, and I knew Nathan's heart was focused on Him. If he could stay that way, we had a shot. It warmed my heart to see my husband taking the leadership role seriously for the first time in years.

CHAPTER 13

The Pines Baptist Church parking lot was packed

like a can of sardines on Sunday morning. Glancing

at my phone as I silenced it, I saw we were about ten

minutes early to service that morning. Looking at

Nathan as he surveyed the parking lot rows, I

noticed him leaning over the steering wheel as he

squinted at the rows of cars.

"Does that help you see?" I asked playfully with a smile.

He laughed and relaxed his tense shoulders back against his seat. "I'm just nervous. So many people we know are going to be bugging us about where we've been for the last four years."

"And the ignored phone calls . . ." I added. Touching his arm, I said, "Maybe they'll just leave us be. You never know."

"Ned won't," he remarked. "I know that guy will be asking."

"It'll be okay," I insisted.

Finding a spot down one of the rows, we parked. As we all got out of the car, Nathan set his Bible on the roof as he adjusted his shirt to tuck it into his pants.

"You sure do look stunning in that dress, Honey," he said, glancing at me as I came around the back bumper. The dress was a yellow summer dress I picked up at a flea market last year.

"Thanks," I replied. The compliment was sweet of him. He knew I spent a couple of hours upstairs getting ready that morning. I just hoped the compliments he gave me would never stop. The affection, the happiness . . . they all made me feel great, but in the back of my mind, I felt it wasn't forever. After all, he did do these things once before and stopped. What would keep him from stopping again? How do we avoid what happened, not only on his part, but my own? These were the questions that haunted my free moments of thought.

"Can I go to service with you and Dad?" Jenny asked as we walked through the parking lot toward the entrance.

Shaking my head gently, I looked at her. "Why

wouldn't you want to go to Youth Group? You always enjoyed it before."

She shrugged. "I don't know. I'm just nervous being here. Felisha and Cindy go here, and I'm not really friends with them at school anymore."

As we came up to the doors, a few of the youth were coming out. A guy and two girls. "Hey, Jenny," the boy said.

"I'm Nathan. Jenny's father," Nathan said firmly as he extended a hand to exchange handshakes with the boy.

"*Dad,*" Jenny said as she went beet red in embarrassment. "I'll catch up with you after church," Jenny said, going with the kids as they walked down the sidewalk to the youth building.

"Who was that boy?" Nathan asked as he watched the kids walk.

"Don't worry about it, dear," I replied, laughing as I linked my arm with his.

With Dakota still by our side, we went into the main foyer of the church. Swarms of people gathered in clusters around laptops that were set up on a table. Seeing past one of the ladies in line, I saw the screen. They were checking in their children to the digitized system. *I don't recall these,* I thought to myself.

Leaning in my ear, Nathan said, "I'll grab us seats in the sanctuary."

As Nathan left in pursuit of seats, I felt a deep peace set over me. Nathan was a good man. I wasn't sure if I'd ever be able to love him the way I did before, but I at least knew my children had a good father and a role model. Sure, he made a mistake, but I'd never tell them.

"Mom," Dakota said, bumping my arm with his elbow.

Turning, I saw he was alerting me to show me I was next in line. I stepped up to the computer to sign Dakota and Jenny into Sunday School.

That evening, I made a needed trip to the store to pick up a gallon of milk and a pizza for the kids and Nathan. After the never ending laundry saga I had going on in the laundry room for the second day in a row, I was too tired to cook. The kids and Nathan loved pizza anyway, so they didn't complain. When I pulled into the driveway back at home that evening, I noticed the living room lights were off. *Strange.* Taking the gallon of milk in one hand and the pizza in the other, I ventured up the driveway and to the

front door. It was open.

"Hello?" I said, stepping into the dimly lit living

room. The hallway light came on and Jenny came

down the stairs.

"Hey, Mom. I'll take that. Dakota and I are upstairs

doing a Bible study guide that Kurt gave me."

"Kurt?" I asked, perplexed as I handed her the pizza.

"Yeah. The guy from church today? Remember? He

was in my Biology class last year."

I nodded. "Okay. Where's your father?"

She smiled and looked toward the kitchen. "Out

back. He's waiting for you." Turning, she hurried

back up the stairs and into her room. Setting my

purse down on the counter, I went over to the

sliding glass door and saw the fire pit ablaze outside.

Opening the door, I stepped outside and went down

the steps to the backyard. Near the fire pit was a small table with a rose lying across the center, but no Nathan. Peering across the moonlit yard, I saw no signs of him. "Nathan?" I asked into the darkness.

"Right here," he replied, coming around the corner with a plate of steak. "Sorry. I didn't know you'd be back this quickly." He set the plate of meat down on the table and pulled out a chair. "Your chair, ma'am."

I smiled and took a seat.

"Just a moment, and I will return with our meals." Taking the plate of steak, he went inside. Seeing the rose again, I picked it up. It was real. Bringing the petals to my nose, I breathed in the aroma of the rose and grinned. *When did he have time to get this?* Looking over at the crackling fire not far from our table, I knew he built it specifically for me. When we were younger, we'd sit outside in the summer and watch the stars while sipping on cups of coffee. I'd always have a blanket wrapped around me or make him build a fire. Even if the temps were in the sixties at night, I'd always have some source of heat to help keep me just a little bit warmer.

Hearing the door open, I glanced over to see Nathan return with two plates in hand. As he set my plate of food down in front of me, my smile grew. He really was trying. The steak looked perfect, and the salad too. "This looks amazing, honey," I said as he took a seat across from me.

"Good." Folding his hands together, he bowed. I joined him. He prayed, "Dear Heavenly Father, we come to you this evening and ask a blessing on the food. May it bring nourishment to our bodies. Let us remember that You alone, God, are the one who can restore the broken-hearted. It's through Your power, mercy and grace that we can find life and joy and peace and happiness. I pray these things in Your name. Amen."

"And bless the cook. Amen," I added.

Looking up from the blessing on the food, I saw Nathan. Not the sinner of a man who had done the unspeakable, but my husband. The real Nathan, who loved me like crazy. Setting his fork down, he reached a hand across the table, palm up. "I love you, Lizzy."

"I love you too," I replied, placing my hand in his.

"I want you to know that I'm not doing all of this just because I'm trying to make up to you. Well, okay, that too." He let out a short laugh before continuing. With my hand still in his, he said, "I'm never going to stop loving you the way I should—

ever again. It doesn't matter what happens. I won't ever let myself get comfortable and take you for granted. Every moment I spend with you is a gift from God. I know it's something that *should* have been there all along, but it wasn't."

"I messed up too, Nathan," I added. "I know what you mean."

He nodded and released my hand. Picking his fork and knife up, he smiled across the table at me and I smiled back. Counseling didn't feel needed in a perfect moment like this one, but I knew we had to do everything possible if we were going to have a chance.

CHAPTER 14

Usually, I was the one who would take a long time

to get ready to go anywhere. Not this time. Instead

of me spending an hour on my hair and another

thirty minutes on what to wear, I was ready in

twenty minutes flat. Today, none of the outward

appearances mattered. What was important was

preparing my heart for marriage counseling down at

Pines Baptist. We'd be meeting with the associate pastor, Tom, a man we've known for years. What would I say? How much information and detail would we need to go into about Nathan's trespasses and my own? I wasn't sure of the answers, but that didn't stop me from repeating the questions in my mind while I waited for Nathan to finish getting ready. Sitting with my feet curled up under me on the couch downstairs in the living room, I ran the questions in my mind over and over again.

To me, marriage counseling was like admitting I didn't know what I was doing, almost like a dirty little piece of laundry you don't want to air. 'We screwed up' and 'we're not sure what to do now' were the statements I didn't want to say. Those kinds of sentences echoed the reality of our marriage. I loved the idea of getting help for Nathan and me, but that didn't mean I wanted people to know my business.

A sigh came from the stairs as Nathan came down them. Glancing over the back of the couch, I looked at his wide-eyed expression. "You ready?" he asked as he came down and into the living room.

"Yep. Ready as I'll ever be," I replied. Standing up, I slipped on my flip-flops and picked up my purse. Walking over to the door, Nathan held it open for me.

In the church parking lot, Nathan grabbed my hand. I didn't pull away. Instead, I just squeezed. We went inside and down the hallway where the associate pastor's office was. As the open door made its way into our view, I could feel my heart begin to pound.

He's going to look at us with disappointment. I just

know it. Before we made it all the way down the hall,

I stopped and pulled on Nathan's hand.

"Do we *have* to do this?" I asked, pleading with my

eyes for this to be over.

Nathan turned his head and looked down the

hallway and then back at me. Releasing my hand

from his, he took a step closer and put his hands on

my arms. Softly, he said, "Elizabeth. I love you, and I

want to *never* hurt you the way I already have. God's

design for marriage was meant for something

beautiful." He shook his head as he continued, "I, in

my sin, made it ugly. We need help getting back on

track with God." He glanced at the door down the

hall. "Tom's going to help direct us. I know you're

worried, but don't be. I'll be there with you. We'll do

it together."

Nathan's words helped ease the pounding in my chest. He was right. We needed the help, and Tom was kind enough to meet with us. He took my hand, and we continued to the door.

As Nathan raised a hand and pushed open the door, Pastor Tom took his glasses off and stood up from behind the desk. A tall, slender man in his early sixties, he carried the type of smile that made you comfortable. Coming around the corner of his desk, he greeted us with handshakes. "It's good to see you two. Come in and have a seat," he said, walking back around his desk.

As I sat down in a chair in front of his desk, my heart couldn't help but race in anticipation of the conversation we were about to have. I knew his wife, Milly, well, and I was sure she would hear all about

Nathan and me tonight. Pressing on my mind in that moment was the verse that Serenah had given me. *Cast all your anxiety on him because he cares for you.* Committing my anxiety over the situation at hand to the Lord, I let myself relax. This man across the desk wasn't just any person in the world. He was a man of Christ, a fellow follower of His Word. If there was anyone Nathan and I should talk to, it was most likely Pastor Tom.

"Let's pray," Pastor Tom said, bowing his head. Nathan and I both bowed our heads. "Lord, we ask you to please bless our time together today. May Your wisdom and hand be over it. Help us all to see Your truth and open our hearts. In Your precious name, Amen." As we lifted our heads, the pastor looked at me and then over at Nathan. "So how are you?" he asked.

"Good. Good," Nathan replied.

Pastor Tom smiled warmly and looked at both of us. "Yeah?"

I reached over and touched Nathan's arm, hoping to help him relax. Looking at him and then over at the Pastor, I said, "We need help. Our marriage is . . . in trouble."

Nathan dipped his chin for a moment and then adjusted in his seat. "We aren't sure what to do, Pastor. We're focused on God now, and we're trying to get right with Him."

"Well, that's a really good start," Tom replied as he reached for his Bible on the desk. "What seems to be the problem then?"

"Things have happened . . ." I said, but he raised his hand.

"You don't need to go into detail with me. That's

between you two and the Lord. I've never seen a case where I needed the gritty details of the issues." He opened up his Bible to a specific part that appeared to be marked off with a paper. "Do you guys mind if I read you something?" he asked, looking up from the Scriptures.

"Please do," Nathan said.

Placing his glasses on, he leaned in and pressed his finger against the page. "Above all, love each other deeply, because love covers over a multitude of sins. 1 Peter 4:8." Peering up at Nathan and then over at me, he raised his eyebrows at us and then leaned back in his chair. "The way I like to look at the Bible is that God doesn't put anything in there that's not important. Loving deeply is the key here in this passage. What do you two think?"

I nodded as I felt my soul stir at the words. He was

right. Love was the answer.

Nathan shook his head and said, "There's respect that is needed also, though." He leaned over the desk and looked at the Bible, "I know respect is mentioned in there too. Not just love."

"True, Nathan," Tom replied. Leaning forward, he said, "Really, why can't respect *be* part of loving deeply?" Tom flipped through his Bible to another area as he continued speaking. "My wife and I have been married for forty-three years, and we still need God in our marriage every day. Without being connected to the vine of Christ, we're hopelessly destined for failure in this life. Marriage is extremely difficult with God. Without Him, it's impossible."

"Did you guys ever get close to divorce?" Nathan asked.

"Nathan!" I scolded him.

"It's okay," Tom replied gently. "Yes. We did. It was right after I retired. We weren't used to being around each other that much . . ." Tom paused for a moment and looked over at a picture of Milly on his desk and then shook his head. "It was ridiculous there for a few months."

"What did you do?" I asked.

Tom looked at Nathan and then at me and said, "We stopped trying to fix it and let God take the wheel."

The words resonated, but still lacked the exact instruction I longed for. Leaning forward, I pressed my hand flat against the desk and asked, "But what does that mean? What did you do?"

"I prayed, read my Bible, and kept focusing on God and my spouse. Over time, it worked out. God did the heavy lifting once I let Him." The pastor turned his eyes back to his Bible and flipped a few more pages until he stopped. Looking up at me and then over to Nathan, he said, "I've seen a lot of people come through that door over there. Often, it's only one spouse, and that's really hard. Sometimes, it's two, but one is only there because they were dragged in . . . but you two." He shook his head and smiled. "You'll be fine. You are both here—that alone shows something. Let's see here." His eyes went down to the Scriptures.

I pulled my hand off the desk and let it fall to my side. Nathan's hand found mine, and my heart warmed at his touch.

Tom read again. "Though one may be overpowered, two can defend themselves. A cord of three strands is not quickly broken. Ecclesiastes 4:12." He looked up at us and continued, "It's not just Nathan and Elizabeth. It's God, Nathan and Elizabeth. Your marriage relationship is with God also. It's hard to remember that when we aren't focused on Him and His truths found in the Bible. You said you started getting back on track with God just recently?"

Nathan nodded and brought his hands together in his lap. "I haven't been leading my family in the Lord these last few years. I've failed." He looked over at me with tears welling in his eyes, then looked over at the pastor. "I have failed them."

"Nathan," Tom said in a warm tone. "That's why you need God in your marriage and in your life. It's not supposed to be up to you alone to handle it all. Look at Adam and Eve in the garden. Before the fall, God walked with Adam and taught him in the garden. The design of God was for Him to have a relationship with us. It's about Him being the object of our worship. When we fade away from God, the

Bible and our prayer lives, we are feeding our sinful flesh side. The Bible says we reap whatever we sow."

Nathan wiped his eyes and kept nodding. "I know. I'm going to be better."

"And you will fail," Tom replied. Looking over at me, he said, "Both of you will keep failing, but you will also succeed in some ways. You just have to keep pushing forward and serving God with your life. This life we have is a process of becoming holy. Though Christ is the redeemer, it's up to us to have a relationship with God. Without a relationship, we'll always be lacking and trying to find fulfillment in this world, and we know what the world offers can never satisfy our need."

The pastor's words cut through all the hurt and spoke directly to me. It wasn't me who was going to fix this disaster of a marriage, and it wasn't Nathan either. It was God. Through time and focusing our attention on the Lord, this could really work. After our meeting with the pastor that day, we decided to forego more counseling and instead joined a marriage class Tom recommended called *Love and Respect*. It was held Tuesday nights at the Fosters' house—a couple from Pines Baptist.

CHAPTER 15

Days passed without an issue between Nathan and

me after our meeting with Pastor Tom. We woke up   '

in the mornings and spent our time together reading

out of the Bible, starting in Galatians. Then Nathan

spent the rest of his days out looking for a job. He

turned in applications, went to hiring events, and

even landed an interview at a company for the

upcoming Friday. It had been three days since the

counseling session at church, and I decided to take

Jenny to the mall. We would shop and then grab a

bite of food for our mother-daughter date of sorts.

After shopping, as we went to sit down with our

food, I saw Derek. My emotions inside went crazy.

Turning quickly with my tray in hand and my

daughter by my side, I did my best to avoid eye

contact with him and went to sit down.

By the time we had finished with lunch and were

dumping our trays, I had forgotten all about him.

"Elizabeth?" Derek asked from behind me.

I froze. My heart raced, and I could feel my face turn

red as my daughter looked behind me at him.

Turning around, I said, "Hi."

"I thought that was you. We miss you back at the

bookstore. How have you been?"

"Who's this?" Jenny asked.

"I'm Derek," he said, extending a hand. "Old co-worker of your mom's."

He said the name that had caused so much turmoil, so much pain in my life for three years of my marriage. *She's going to tell Nathan . . . Great,* I thought. Everything was going to fall apart. My verse suddenly came to me. *Cast all your anxiety on him because he cares for you.* I had to trust God.

Nodding, I said, "We've gotta get home. Nathan is waiting for us." Placing my hand behind Jenny's back, I led her away a bit forcefully, so on our way through the mall, she turned to me.

"What's your deal, Mom? You were acting so strangely with that man."

"Nothing, honey," I replied as I hastened my steps toward the exit. In almost a continuous prayer, I asked for God's hand to be over the situation.

Arriving home, Jenny darted up the stairs and into her room with her bags of clothing. She didn't tell Nathan about Derek, which I was thankful for, but I had a decision to make. I could tell Nathan what happened and just lay it all out, or I could hide it and hope Jenny said nothing. Then I let out a sigh of relief.

I was done hiding.

If our relationship was going to be founded on God, I needed to trust in Him fully. Trust He is God and He decides on the outcome. "We need to talk," I said, looking at Nathan on the couch.

"Okay," he replied with wide eyes.

"Don't worry. Let's go out back."

"All right," he replied. Standing up, he handed me a letter. "The invite for Serenah and Charlie next month."

"Awesome," I replied, taking it from him and tossing it on the counter. We continued outside and into the grass of the backyard. Taking his hands in mine, I said, "First off—I saw Derek today at the mall. I kept the conversation short and ended it quickly."

He furrowed his eyebrows.

Touching his arm, I said, "Don't worry about it, Nathan. Anyway, I realized something about myself that I didn't know before. When I kept the biopsy from you, I was essentially playing God. I made the decision not to tell you, like you didn't need that in your life." Stepping in closer, I framed his face with my hands. "I love you, Nathan. I've come to a decision."

"What?" he asked, confused.

"I've made up my mind about us." He dipped his chin, but I lifted it with my hands and smiled. "I can't promise I won't ever randomly break down crying or be irrational at times, but what I can promise you is that I will love you the rest of my life."

Leaning in, he smoothed his hand over my hair and pushed a strand behind my ear, then kissed me. His lips pressed against mine, and I felt all my vulnerability rush through me, but with it came love. Though we had a long path ahead of us still, I knew I made the right decision.

Decisions. They shape us into who we are and impact our lives in ways we often never realize.

When I married Nathan, I married my best friend—

that was easy. When I made the decision to stay

with him, I chose to stay with an imperfect person

just like me. If it weren't for God and His Spirit

within me, I wouldn't have had the strength to stay.

I had every reason in the world to leave Nathan, but

in the end, I made the decision to stay and trust

God.

The End.

Did you enjoy the Book?

Please
Leave a Review

BOOK PREVIEW

Preview of "Amongst the Flames"

Prologue

Fire. Four letters, two vowels and one reaction.

That reaction depends on who you are. For me and the fellas at Station 9 in downtown Spokane, our reaction is one of quickness, speed and precision. A few seconds delay could mean someone's life. We don't have time to think, only do. And we don't do this for the recognition or because it's just some job, we do it because this is what we were born to do. My resume, if I had one, would only say one thing on it: Firefighter. I'm one of those guys that you don't really think about unless something has gone terribly wrong. Usually it's when your house is on fire.

I won't bore you with the countless calls where we just show up with our lights on and we're just there to support the police and ambulance. I'm sure you've seen us sitting across the street quietly once or twice while they wheel Mrs. Johnson out on a gurney to the ambulance at three o'clock in the morning. I also won't explain to you the hundred calls a year we get on burning popcorn in a kitchen. No. This story I'm going to share with you is not only about the worst fire I had ever seen in my life, but it'll also encompass how important God is, not only in marriage, but in life.

This is not a story you'll find on the front page of your local newspaper while you're sipping your morning cup of coffee. You also won't catch it on the ten o'clock news. Nope. Instead, it's a story that will inspire you to look at life differently and challenge you to believe that with God even the worst fire you face is nothing in comparison with His power, grace and mercy.

Belief in God is not really an option for me when I run into burning buildings to save lives. It's a core fundamental building block of who I am. I won't sit here and tell you that I'm a perfect Christian though; that would be a lie. Soon enough, you'll read about my plethora of issues and flaws amongst the pages that follow. What I will do is stay true to the truth the best that I can. I'm not telling this story to make a record of my sins or those of others. I'm giving you this story to give you hope. Hope of a brighter tomorrow that you can look forward to, hope of a world where acceptance isn't only preached, but it's applied alongside the scriptures to our lives.

I am Cole Taylor and this is my story.

Chapter 1

Walking down an aisle in the grocery store with

Kane, Micah and Greg one morning at about eight o'clock I couldn't help but laugh a little. I caught Kane checking out a pretty brunette a few aisles over in the bakery.

"Always on the prowl, aren't ya?" I asked, smiling over at him. Kane was the station's notorious single twenty-three-year-old male with nothing but women on his mind. He once admitted to me that he bought a full set of turnouts online from an ex-fireman just so he could suit up in a full fireman outfit for a girl.

"She's cute," Kane replied with a half-grin on his face. He shot another look over at her and his smile grew.

"Maybe she can bake you a cake or something?" Greg said with a soft but sarcastic tone as he grabbed a box of pasta from the shelf. Greg was one of the quieter guys on the crew.

Micah and I erupted in laughter. Kane smiled and said, "I'm sure there's more to her than that."

"How would you even know that?" I asked.

He shrugged. "It's a hunch, I know about these things."

"Well, at least you know she has a sweet side," Micah added. Kane laughed a little as he pushed the cart down towards the end of the aisle.

On the way over to the meat section of the store, a man with furrowed eyebrows made a beeline for us. Leaning into Kane's ear, I said, "Move the cart out of his way." Kane did, but it didn't help. The elderly gentleman shifted his footing to line up with our cart as he continued towards us.

Arriving at us, the man latched his worn hands to each side of our cart and demanded in a sharp tone, "What are you doing here?"

"Same as most people here, just grocery shopping... you?" Kane asked, crossing his arms as he released his grip from the cart.

"Are you on the clock right now?" the man asked. He shot a quick look at each of us individually as if we were caught in some kind of predicament.

"Yeah," I replied, stepping in front of Kane and up to the gentleman. I knew I needed to get between them before Kane did something stupid. His fuse was short when it came to people who didn't respect firefighters. For instance, there was a call one time that Kane and I were on where the man whose house was on fire started complaining to us about how long it took us to respond. Kane took his revenge inside the home when he used the butt of his axe to smash the guy's big screen TV.

"Is there a problem going on in the store we should know about?" Micah asked, looking over my shoulder at the man. Micah was my best friend at the station and he was always looking for the best in people no matter what the situation appeared to be.

"Yeah, matter of fact there is a problem ya chump! And I'm looking right at it," he shouted, raising his hands from the cart. I looked back at Kane as I knew the comment would set him off. Catching his gaze before he said anything, I could see Kane trying to keep his mouth shut. That little stunt he pulled at that fire by smashing the guy's TV landed him with a suspension without pay.

Micah raised his hands. "We're just trying to get to some supplies, Sir."

"Yeah– he's right. We don't want any trouble, Sir. We need to keep moving." I grabbed onto the cart and began walking past the disgruntled citizen.

"This is how my tax dollars is spent, huh?" He asked as he laughed sarcastically, shaking his head at us.

"I'm filing a complaint with your station!" he said from behind us. He must have been looking at the back of our fleece pullovers as he continued,

"Station 9... Who's in charge over there?"

"Thomas Sherwood and Sean Hinley are our Captains and Paul Jensen's the Chief," I said over my shoulder to him.

"I'll be calling them right away!" he shouted.

We all three managed to keep our cool and made it over to the meats. As we came up to the bunker with steaks and stopped, Kane said, "We risk our lives, yet people still find a reason to complain... What is with that?" He glanced back at the angry man as he now appeared to be arguing with a grocery store worker.

I turned to Kane. "Do you do this job because you want people to think you're a hero?"

"No..." he replied softly. "But that kind of thing just isn't right."

"No, it's not right," I agreed. "But we don't do this to impress people, Kane. You know that. We do this job because it's our duty and we do it to protect the people of Spokane. We serve them, no matter how poorly we get treated."

"Cole's right, man," Micah said with a nod. "We can't let people like him get in our head."

"We can't let them undermine our reasons for doing

this," Greg added.

"I find honor in what we do and someone like that just bugs me."

"I know it does," I replied, putting a hand on his shoulder. "And thank you for not saying anything to him." I turned back to the steaks. "What cut do we want boys?" I asked.

Suddenly dispatch came over all our radios for a fire at the Canyon Creek Apartments on South Westcliff. We all four began sprinting for the front doors. My heart began pounding as adrenaline coursed through every one of my veins. Weaving between the aisles and shopping carts, we made our way outside. Spotting a cart boy on the way through the parking lot, I stopped and told him about our cart in the back of the store. He thanked me and I headed over to the truck.

Micah jumped into the driver seat. He was the ladder company's engineer and that meant the man behind the wheel. Greg sat up front with Micah; his role varied and depended much on what was needed on each call. Kane and I were the guys who did search and rescue, cut power and helped with ventilation cuts on the roof.

As Kane and I suited up in the back, Kane asked, "Did you see that chick in the bakery look concerned as we dashed out of there?"

I laughed. "No, didn't catch that," I said, pulling up my suspenders across the front of my chest.

"When we go back later I'm going to go talk to her. Bet I can get those digits," he replied as he slid his Nomax head and neck protector over his eyes. "I'll for sure get her number."

"She could be married," I replied.

"Nah, I saw her left hand when she was putting out donuts in the window earlier."

I laughed. "Wait... what ever happened to that Heidi girl? I almost completely forgot about her."

"He got bored of her," Micah said over his shoulder to us. "He can't seem to stay interested in one gal; you know that."

"Shouldn't you be keeping your eyes on the road?" Kane retorted.

"Really though, man, what happened?" I asked, looking over at Kane.

"Just didn't work out," Kane said as he shrugged.

We slowed down as we arrived at the scene. Glancing out my window, I could see the fire had already engulfed much of the apartment complex and I felt another surge of adrenaline. I was excited and yet terrified out of my mind of the unknown that lay before me. It was that way every time we got a call.

Glancing at the other fire truck on scene, I saw Thomas Sherwood, the shift captain of station 9 and my father-in-law. He was already on scene along with the other guys who rode over on the engine truck. They were already about done hooking up the hose to the hydrant as we came to a complete stop. Leaping from my seat, my feet barely hit the pavement before the captain reached me.

"We need a grab on the second floor," he shouted. "There's a four year old girl in apartment one-forty-two." My heart felt like it skipped a beat as I looked up at the roaring flames. Saving lives wasn't anything new for me, but I never could get used to it. Even after ten years of service, every time lives were at stake, it was difficult, especially when the lives of children were involved.

"Got it," I replied as I grabbed my oxygen tank from the side of the truck and secured it onto my back. Grabbing my axe and Halligan bar, I turned as I pulled my mask over my face and put on my helmet. A hand on my shoulder stopped me from heading directly to the building.

"And, Cole," the captain said as I turned around.

"Yeah?" I asked.

"Be careful in there, I don't have the energy to explain to my daughter how her husband died today."

"No worries, you haven't had to yet," I replied. Turning, I looked at the apartment entrance and saw the black smoke billowing out the front door. I jogged up to the door and as I entered, I saw Rick, starting the exterior attack on the fire from outside with his hose in hand. He was spraying down the

nearby building so it would not catch on fire. I gave

him a nod. Rick Alderman was one of the veterans '

on the crew. It was he, Micah and I for the past ten

years at fire station 9. Kane came on a couple years

after me and the others all were fairly new, each

under five years. The older vets from the old days

when I first started —like Hillman and Conrad—

moved away and transferred to other stations. But

no matter who came or went, when we were on the

scene we were like that of a brotherhood. No man

left behind, ever.

Coming inside the burning building, I immediately

noticed the extreme temperatures inside. It wasn't

typical, a bit warmer than I was used to. I pushed

the sensation of being trapped in a furnace out of

my mind as I ventured in further. I trekked through

the black smoke and up the stairs in search for the child. My jacket was failing to keep the high temperatures of the heat from my skin and the burning was digging in. Ignoring common-sense reactions to extreme situations is a requirement that they don't advertise in the job description. Who in his right mind after all would run into a burning building, on purpose?

My visibility was low at the top of the stairs inside. The charcoal-black smoke was thick and filled every square inch. Seeing a door within reach, I came up to it. Squinting, I could see it read 'one forty four.' It wasn't the one I needed. I trudged through the ever-thickening smoke as the heat gnawed at my skin until I found the apartment I needed. One-forty-two. Relieved, I grabbed for the door knob, but found it locked. Taking a few steps back, I launched a kick to the door that would have impressed an MMA fighter, but it wasn't enough to make it budge. I brought my Halligan front side and stuck it right between the door and the frame. My skin continued to burn from the heat and my muscles screamed in pain as I pried open the door. Finally, it budged open.

Stepping through the smoke filled room, I shouted, "Fire department, Call out!" The sound of the roaring flames and falling pieces of debris made it nearly impossible to hear anything else.

Lowering myself to the floor, I moved through the living room and reached a doorway. An explosion suddenly came from another part of the building. Covering my helmet, I braced myself for any falling debris. Continuing through the doorway and smoke, I noticed a smoldering teddy bear next to me. This must be the girl's room, I thought to myself as I raised my head to survey the room. Trying to see through the smoke was difficult, but I spotted a closet across the floor. I repeated, "Fire department, Call out!" as I inched my way over to the closet. Getting to the closet, I found the little girl almost about to lose consciousness. Ripping my mask off in a frenzy, I shoved it over her face and said, "It is going to be okay, I'm going to get you out of here." She struggled to breathe into the mask. Our breathing apparatuses weren't so easy to use when not properly trained. "Just try to take small and short breaths," I said.

I grabbed the little girl and held her close to my chest in my arms, using myself as a shield as I crawled back towards the doorway. Once back into the living room, I stood up for the rest of the journey out. But before I could reach the front door of the apartment, an explosion came from the kitchen. Covering the girl as much as possible and dropping to the floor, I protected her from the blast. But a piece of metal shot across the room from the explosion and hit me in the upper arm. I thanked God it was only my arm as I regained my footing and continued to the door with the girl. My adrenaline was pumping and my heart was pounding so hard that I had no idea how bad my wound was. As I came to the stairs that led out of the apartment, pain suddenly shot through my arm, sending me collapsing to the top of the stairs.

Lying there I turned my head and looked down to the base of the stairs. I could see through the mostly faded smoke as Kane came rushing through the doorway and up the stairs to me.

Did you enjoy this sample? Go to

www.tkchapin.com and get a copy today!

BOOK PREVIEW

Preview of "The Perfect Cast"

Prologue

Each of us has moments of impact in life.

Sometimes it's in the form of *love*, and sometimes in

the form of *sadness*. It is in these times that our

world changes forever. They shape us, they define

us, and they transform us from the people we once

were into the people we now are.

The summer before my senior year of high

school is one that will live with me forever. My

parents' relationship was on the rocks, my brother

was more annoying than ever, and I was forced to

leave the world I loved and cared about in Seattle. A

summer of change, a summer of growth, and a

summer I'll never forget.

Chapter 1 ~ Jess

Jess leaned her head against the passenger side window as she stared out into the endless fields of wheat and corn. She felt like an alien in a foreign land, as it looked nothing like the comfort of her home back in Seattle.

She was convinced her friends were lucky to not have a mother who insisted on whisking them away to spend the *entirety* of their summer out in the middle of nowhere in Eastern Washington. She would have been fine with a weekend visit, but the entire summer at Grandpa's? That was a bit uncalled for, and downright wrong. Her mother said the trip was so Jess and her brother Henry could spend time with her grandpa Roy, but Jess had no interest in doing any such thing.

On the car ride to Grandpa's farm to be dropped off and abandoned, Jess became increasingly annoyed with her mother. Continually, her mother would glance over at Jess, looking for conversation. Ignoring her mom's attempts to make eye contact with her, Jess kept her eyes locked and staring out the window. Every minute, and every second of the car ride, Jess spent wishing the summer away.

After her mother took the exit off the freeway that led out to the farm, a loud pop came from the driver side tire and brought the car to a grinding halt. Her mom was flustered, and quickly got out of the car to investigate the damage. Henry, Jess's obnoxious and know-it-all ten-year-old brother, leaned between the seats and glanced out the windshield at their mom.

"Stop being so annoying," Jess said, pushing his face back between the seats. He sat back and then began to reach for the door. Jess looked back at him and asked, "What are you doing?"

"I'm going to help Mom."

"Ha. You can't help her; you don't know how to change a tire."

"Well, I am going to *try*." Henry climbed out of the car and shut it forcefully. Jess didn't want this summer to exist and it hadn't even yet begun. If only she could fast forward, and her senior year of high school could start, she'd be happy. But that wasn't the case; there was no remote control for her life. Instead, the next two and half months were going to consist of being stuck out on a smelly farm with Henry and her grandpa. She couldn't stand more than a few minutes with her brother, and being

stuck in a house with no cable and *him*? That was a

surefire sign that one of them wasn't making it

home alive. Watching her mother stare blankly at

the car, unsure of what to do, Jess laughed a little to

herself. *If you wouldn't have left Dad, you would have*

avoided this predicament. Her dad knew how to fix

everything. Whether it was a flat tire, a problematic

science project or her fishing pole, her dad was

always there for her no matter what. That was up

until her mother walked out on him, and screwed

everybody's life up. He left out of the country on a

three month hiatus. Jess figured he had a broken

heart and just needed the time away to process her

mom leaving him in the dust.

Henry stood outside the car next to his

mother, looking intently at the tire. Accidentally

catching eye contact with her mother, Jess rolled her eyes. Henry had been trying to take over as the *man of the house* ever since the split. It was cute at first, even to Jess, but his rule of male superiority became rather old quickly when Henry began telling Jess not to speak to her mother harshly and to pick up her dirty laundry. Taking the opportunity to cut into her mom, Jess rolled down her window. "Why don't you call Grandpa? Oh, that's right... he's probably outside and doesn't have a cell phone... but even if he did, he wouldn't have reception."

"Don't start with me, Jess." Her mother scowled at her. Jess watched as her mother turned away from the car and spotted a rickety, broken down general store just up the road.

Her mom began to walk along the side of the road with Henry. Jess didn't care that she wasn't invited on the family trek along the road. It was far too hot to walk anywhere, plus she preferred the coolness of the air conditioning. She wanted to enjoy the small luxury of air conditioning before getting to her grandpa's, where she knew there was sure to be nothing outside of box fans.

Jess pulled her pair of ear buds out from the front pouch of her backpack and plugged them into her phone. Tapping into her music as she put the ear buds in, she set the playlist to shuffle. Staring back out her window, she noticed a cow feeding on a pile of hay through the pine trees, just over the other side of a barbed wire fence. *I really am in the middle of nowhere.*

Chapter 2 ~ Roy

The blistering hot June sun shone brightly through the upper side of the barn and through the loft's open doorway, illuminating the dust and alfalfa particles that were floating around in the air. Sitting on a hay bale in the upper loft of the barn, Roy watched as his nineteen-year-old farmhand Levi retrieved each bale of hay from the conveyor that sat at the loft's doorway. Each bale of alfalfa weighed roughly ninety pounds; it was a bit heavier than the rest of the grass hay bales that were stored in the barn that year. Roy enjoyed watching his farmhand work. He felt that if he watched him enough, he might be able to rekindle some of the strength that he used to have in his youth.

While Roy was merely watching, that didn't

protect him from the loft's warmth, and sweat quickly began to bead on his forehead. Reaching for his handkerchief from his back pocket, he brought it to his forehead and dabbed the sweat. Roy appreciated the help of Levi for the past year. Whether it was feeding and watering the cattle, fixing fences out in the fields, or shooting the coyotes that would come down from the hill and attack the cows, Levi was always there and always helping. He was the son of Floyd Nortaggen, the man who ran the dairy farm just a few miles up the road. If it wasn't for Levi, Roy suspected he would have been forced to give up his farm and move into a retirement home. Roy knew retirement homes were places where people went to die, and he just wasn't ready to die. And he didn't want to die in a building full of people that he didn't know; he wanted to die out on his farm, where he always felt he belonged.

"Before too long, I'll need you to get up on the roof and get those shingles replaced. I'm afraid one good storm coming through this summer could ruin the hay."

Levi glanced up at the roof as he sat on the final bale of hay he had stacked. Wiping away the sweat from his brow with his sleeve, he looked over to Roy. "I'm sure I could do that. How old are the shingles?"

A deep smile set into Roy's face as he thought about when he and his father had built the barn back when he was just a boy. "It's been forty years now." His father had always taken a fancy to his older brother, but when his brother had gone away on a mission trip for the summer, his dad had

relied on Roy for help with constructing the barn.

Delighted, he'd spent the summer toiling in the heat

with his dad. He helped lay the foundation, paint

the barn and even helped put on the roof. Through

sharing the heat of summer and sips of lemonade

that his mother would bring out to them, Roy and

his father grew close, and remained that way until

his father's death later in life.

"Forty years is a while... my dad re-shingled

his barn after twenty."

"Shingles usually last between twenty and

thirty years." Roy paused to let out a short laugh.

"I've been pushing it for ten. Really should have

done it last summer when I first started seeing the

leaks, but I hadn't the strength and was still too

stubborn to accept your help around here."

"I imagine it's quite difficult to admit needing help. I don't envy growing old –no offense."

"None taken," Roy replied, glancing over his shoulder at the sound of a car coming up the driveway over the bridge. "I believe my grandchildren have arrived."

"I'll be on my way then; I don't want to keep you, and it seems to me we are done here."

"Thank you for the help today. I'll write your check, but first get the hay conveyor equipment put away. Just come inside the farmhouse when you're done."

Roy climbed down the ladder and Levi followed behind him. As Roy exited the barn doors, he could see his daughter faintly behind the reflection of the sun off the windshield of her silver

Prius. Love overcame him as he made eye contact

with her. His daughter was the apple of his eye, and

he felt she was the only thing he had done right in

all the years of his life on earth. He'd never admit it

to anyone out loud, but Tiff was his favorite child.

She was the first-born and held a special place in his

heart. The other kids gravitated more to their

mother anyway; Tiffany and he were always close.

Parking in front of the garage that matched

the paint of the barn, red with white trim, His

daughter Tiffany stepped out of the driver side door

and smiled at him. Hurrying her steps through the

gravel, she ran up to her dad and hugged him as she

let out what seemed to be a sigh of relief.

Watching over her shoulder as Jess got out of

the car, Roy saw her slam the door. He suspected the

drive hadn't gone that well for the three of them, but

did the courtesy of asking without assuming. "How was the drive?"

"You don't want to ask..." she replied, glancing back at Jess as her daughter lingered near the corner of the garage.

Roy smiled. "I have a fresh batch of lemonade inside," he said, trying to lighten the tension he could sense. Seeing Henry was still in the backseat fiddling with something, Roy went over to one of the back doors and opened the door.

"Hi Grandpa," Henry said, looking up at him.

Leaning his head into the car, Roy smiled. "I'm looking for Henry, have you seen him? Because there's no way you are, Henry! He's just a little guy." Roy used his hand to show how tall Henry *should be* and continued, "About this tall, if my memory serves me correctly."

Henry laughed. "Stop Grandpa! It's me, I'm Henry!"

"I know... I'm just playing with you, kiddo! I haven't seen you in years! You've grown like a weed! Give your ol' Grandpa a hug!" Henry dropped his tablet on the seat and climbed over a suitcase of Jess's to embrace his grandpa in a warm hug.

"Can we go fishing Grandpa? Can we go today?"

Roy laughed as he stood upright. "Maybe tomorrow. The day is going to be over soon and I'd like to visit with your mother some."

Henry dipped his chin to his chest as he sighed. "Okay." Reaching into the back trunk area of the car, Henry grabbed his backpack and then scooted off his seat and out from the car. Just then, Jess let out a screech, which directed everyone's attention over to her at the garage.

"A mouse, are you kidding me?" With a look of disgust, she stomped off around Levi's truck, and down the sidewalk that led up to the farmhouse.

"Aren't you forgetting something?" Tiffany asked, which caused Jess to stop in her tracks. She turned around and put her hand over her brow to shield the sun.

"What, mom?"

"Your suitcases... maybe?" Tiffany replied with a sharp tone.

Roy placed a hand on Tiffany's shoulder. "That's okay. Henry and I can get them."

"No. Jess needs to get them." Roy could tell that his daughter was attempting to draw a line in the sand. A line that Roy and his late wife Lucille had drawn many times with her and the kids.

"Really, Mom?" Jess asked, placing a hand on her hip. "Those suitcases are heavy; the men should carry them. Grandpa is right."

Henry tugged on his mother's shirt corner. "I think you should let this one go, Mother." He smiled and nodded to Roy. "Grandpa and I have it."

Tiffany shook her head and turned away from Jess as she went to the back of the car. "She's so difficult, Dad. I hate it," Tiffany said, slapping the trunk. "She doesn't understand how life really works."

"Winnie," Roy replied. "Pick your battles."

The nickname *Winnie* came from when she was three years old. She would wake up in the middle of the night, push a chair up to the pantry and sneak the honey back into her bedroom. On several occasions, they would awaken the next day to find her snuggling an empty bottle of honey underneath her covers.

"I know. It's just hard sometimes, because everything is a battle with her lately."

Did you enjoy this preview?

Pick up a copy of **The Perfect Cast** *today!*

OTHER BOOKS

Diamond Lake Series

One Thursday Morning (Book 1)

One Friday Afternoon (Book 2)

One Saturday Evening (Book 3) *September 2016*

Embers & Ashes Series

One Friday Afternoon

Amongst the Flames (Book 1)

Out of the Ashes (Book 2)

Up in Smoke (Book 3)

After the Fire (Book 4)

Love's Enduring Promise Series

The Perfect Cast (Book 1)

Finding Love (Book 2)

Claire's Hope (Book 3)

Dylan's Faith (Book 4)

Stand Alones

Love Again

Love Interrupted

A Chance at Love

The Lost Truth

Visit www.tkchapin.com for all the latest releases

Subscribe to the Newsletter for special

Prices, free gifts and more!

www.tkchapin.com

ABOUT THE AUTHOR

T.K. CHAPIN writes Christian Romance books designed to inspire and tug on your heart strings. He believes that telling stories of faith, love and family help build the faith of Christians and help non-believers see how God can work in the life of believers. He gives all credit for his writing and storytelling ability to God. The majority of the novels take place in and around Spokane Washington, his hometown. Chapin makes his home in the Pacific Northwest and has the pleasure of raising his daughter with his beautiful wife Crystal. To find out more about T.K. Chapin or his books, visit his website at www.tkchapin.com.

Made in the USA
San Bernardino, CA
21 March 2017